IF YOU LOVE ME

CIARA KNIGHT

If You Love Me
Book I
Sugar Maple Series
Copyright ©2020 by Ciara Knight
All rights reserved.

Cover art ©2020 by Yocla Cover Designs
Edited by Bev Katz Rosenbaum
Copy Edit by Rachel
****To receive a FREE starter library (Two free books) AND an alert of Ciara's next book releases, go to Ciara's Exclusive Reader group at www.ciaraknight.com/newsletter. ****

✿ Created with Vellum

READER LETTER

Dear Friends,

You have been requesting a new sweet, small town series for a while, so I am happy to share Sugar Maple with you! Per your requests, this will have the feel of a Sweetwater County book, but with all new characters, a new town, and new situations.

I tend to find inspiration for my stories in everyday life and this first book is no different. IF YOU LOVE ME developed into a story by watching several local businesses shut down in my town due to economic issues or by being pushed out by larger chain stores. The few mom and pop stores that have survived struggle daily to remain open. Since I'm a lover of all things small town, genuine, good, and loving, I hope to see a resurgence of small businesses in my own area.

I hope you enjoy Carissa Donahue's journey to save her small bakery, the man who enters her life and challenges her to want more, and that you fall in love with the town elders the way that I have. Be careful, you don't want to get on Davey's bad side or you might be Tar and Southernized. You'll have to read IF YOU LOVE ME to understand, but once you do, I know you'll agree with me about one thing-Sugar Maple is a place where your home and heart belong.

Ciara Knight

CHAPTER ONE

CARISSA DONAHUE STOOD at the floor-to-ceiling windows of Mayor Horton's office, hoping to see Jacqueline Ramor cross the town square before she entered Sugar Maple Town Hall. Carissa needed more than a moment, though, to face the stylish-boyfriend-stealing-Judas Jackie. After all, even a decade hadn't soothed the wounds of a friend's betrayal.

Despite no sign of Judas below, Carissa remained at her perfect vantage point to see the town goings-on. That was probably why Mayor Horton always knew town business and why the mayor's office had this prime spot. Carissa spotted one of her four childhood besties, Felicia, remove the last poinsettia from the foot of the Sugar Maple, Tennessee sign. Sensible Felicia, the negotiator of the group, placed the last of the over one hundred flowers that had decorated the town for the holidays on a cart. The cart squeaked, the sound echoing up to the third story window where Carissa stood, and the negotiator headed toward the courthouse for their meeting, undoubtedly to, well...negotiate a partnership of sorts.

Frost crusted the edges of glass near the faded white window molding. Carissa didn't like the cold, sleet-covered, brown grass winter. Everyone saw January as the beginning. She saw it as an end.

The memories of dinner ten years ago threatened to darken her mood, but she pushed the anger and resentment away. January was a difficult enough month to face. The month she wished they could skip. The first month of the year meant the end of her busiest season, the end of holiday cheer, and the end of her relationship with the man she was supposed to grow old with.

Carissa glanced around the open square one last time for Judas Jackie, but there was no sign of her. It wouldn't be long, though. The once Fabulous Five who ruled the halls of Sugar Maple High School would crowd begrudgingly into Ms. Horton's county office to discuss the scheme to secure the town's future.

The sound of laughter and greetings echoed up the stairs from the entryway, warning that the commotion of past friend-ship turned frenemy was approaching. Carissa rubbed her belly, attempting to free the knots twisting her insides.

There would be snide remarks with a smile and underhanded nudges to provoke arguments, but no one would fully engage in war. Not in front of their childhood mentor, and former teacher, Mayor Horton. Of course, she'd always be Ms. Horton to the five of them and a second mother to Carissa. Especially after taking her in when her parents left her behind.

The woman was a force of power but with a pleasing disposi-tion and a model look to her. She was the only woman who had vibrant sliver hair that made her look young and lively instead of aged.

"Don't look so glum and lost over there, sweet Carissa. We need your expertise. This is going to be an amazing opportunity, not only to revive the economy of the town, but to make your bakery explode with business year-round." Ms. Horton's soothing voice drew Carissa from her moment of self-pity. A place she only allowed herself to dwell in once a year, but even now she didn't like visiting the empty space of loss and regrets.

"I'm not. I just think you're overestimating me and this meeting. You and I both know how this will go." Carissa didn't need to explain. They both knew the proverbial lines that would be drawn in the office with Judas Jackie and Southern Belle Mary-Beth on one side, and Carissa and Sassy Stella on the other, with the negotiator Felicia firmly planted in the center.

Stella marched into the room with her tied-back, crow-colored hair sticking out in puffs around her ears. She joined Carissa on the far side as if an X marked her spot by Carissa's side. She crossed her blue overall-clad arms as an armor against what was yet to come. She was Carissa's Judas Jackie shield.

"Maybe she thinks this is a waste of time. Time we could be spending working and earning money to survive instead of fantasizing about some rich producer deciding to bless us with his all-mighty presence," Stella said in her sassy tone with a thickened Latina accent she reserved for special combative opportunities.

"I have to agree with Stella. Not in the same words, mind you." Carissa tucked her hair behind her ear and drew in a bitter breath. "It's just that we all know that you concocted this plan not just to save the town but to bring us girls together. You succeeded in doing that. Jackie opened the dress store, so she'll be staying, and Mary-Beth opened the coffee shop. Not to mention that Felicia's plant nursery is doing well. See, you got all five of us back home."

"Geographically you're close, but fences haven't been mended." Ms. Horton tsked. "And all because of a stupid boy."

Her words sent a winter blast through Carissa. Ms. Horton never understood that her life had been shattered that day. Not from the boy but the betrayal of the friend who took him. That was a sin beyond what any love interest could do to her.

"I disagree." Stella sat uncharacteristically straight with a Cheshire cat smile.

"Really?" Ms. Horton's eyes-wide, mouth-open expression had to match Carissa's own.

Stella shrugged. "Sure. The fence is as strong now as it was the day we met. Barbed wire strewn between white picket fences and roughhewn poles."

She had a point. The first day of kindergarten Jackie had tried to braid Stella's hair and ended up with finger paint down her white dress.

"You don't give yourself enough credit." Ms. Horton rounded her desk in her typical pencil skirt, button-up, and solid two-inch heels. "You aren't so rough around the edges anymore."

"I was thinking that was Jackie, but whatever." Stella shrugged and studied the oil grease under her nails. Good thing Jackie wasn't in the room to point out her flaws.

Ms. Horton patted Stella's arm and then returned to her desk, sliding her glasses on and looking down at her laptop. "You'll have to put your differences aside and work together when the Executive Production Supervisor arrives."

"An executive what?" Stella asked in her best Knox-style tone, despite the fact she was born and raised in Sugar Maple.

Carissa wanted to laugh, but she stifled it at the sound of approaching heavy boot steps that had to be Felicia in her work galoshes. Sure enough, she appeared with Southern Belle Marry-Beth at her side, leaving only Judas to make her fashionably late entrance.

An uneasiness settled in the pit of Carissa's stomach.

Stella cleared her throat as fast as Carissa cleared her grin. "It's five minutes past. I have work to get back to, you know."

Sensible Felicia sat in the cream-colored neutral zone chair she'd claimed since day one of planning this crazy scheme to save little Sugar Maple from bankruptcy. Perhaps growing up in a mixed-race household and learning to navigate the prejudice of an ill-educated network of small-town teens was what molded her into such an amazing peacekeeper. Her features were beyond exotic, but she had never learned to embrace her unique beauty.

"We're only five minutes late. I had to close up shop, and I couldn't throw my customer out. Believe it or not, you're not the only one who has to work to earn a living around here," Mary-Beth said in the sweetest southern tone while she toyed with her earring, which they all knew meant she was nervous. That was the problem with childhood friends turned enemies... There was way too much ammo you could shoot at each other in an argument.

"Wasn't talking about you two," Stella said in a less hostile tone than expected.

"Jacqueline will be here soon." Ms. Horton pressed on with a hint of irritation in her voice. "As I was saying, we need to get organized before the show executive arrives."

Carissa's desire to escape this redundant and hopeless friend-forced meeting kicked up her irritation. "You mean more prepared than November 1st when we spent two days decorating the square with extra carved pumpkins to create the right scene for the production, or do you mean December 19th, when you had us painting pine trees with fake white snow and assembling nutcrackers in the sleet at two in the morning?"

Jacqueline sauntered into the room with a perfected aristocratic snicker. "Wow, look at Ms. Sweet, who never says an ill-word to anyone, channeling her inner Stella."

Felicia shot up from the chair and stood between them. "Great, we're all here now. Let's get started."

Ms. Horton cleared her throat. "I know we've had some setbacks, but this time will be different. In November they had a corporate restructuring, and in December they had to pull it because of taking on a special with Hallmark Movies."

Jackie set her designer handbag down on Ms. Horton's desk and posed with her hip out to one side and her nose in the air. "If you say January is a new year for new things, you're going to send Carissa into a baking frenzy."

Carissa rubbed a smudge of flour from her knuckle. She didn't want Jackie to see she'd already visited Crazy Town baking today, because then she'd know the truth. Her boyfriend runaway move still hurt.

Mary-Beth fidgeted with one of her eight bracelets. The girl loved her jewelry. Somehow she could wear dozens of pieces and still look perfectly put together. "January isn't so bad. It brings snow and hot chocolate."

Carissa couldn't hold it in any longer. "This is the month when everyone's Christmas-spirt-covered lies turn to icing winter truths."

The smile on Jackie's face drove her insides to pre-heat, but when Stella cracked her knuckles, Carissa knew she had to remain calm if for no other reason than to help Ms. Horton. She owed her that much after all she'd done when Carissa was younger, taking her in when her family transferred out of town so that she could remain with her four best friends in high school.

"You're up first, Carissa." Ms. Horton put her arm around Carissa and snugged her close.

"Me?" Her stomach rolled and fizzed and tightened.

"Why would she be up first?" Jackie's snotty, slight-British-wannabe accent made the fizzing turn to a boil. "I mean, we all know that I should be the first spotlight segment on the new Knox Brevard project. I'm the only one with big city experience and corporate clients, and we all know I can keep a man interested."

Stella sat forward, resting her elbows on her knees. "A man-stealing, failed wannabe New York fashionista—"

"Ladies, please. We're getting off topic. The exec requested to meet with the bakers first." Ms. Horton abandoned Carissa's side so that she could keep the peace. The woman was either brave or crazy. When she had her mind set on something, though, she was like a dog with a prime rib bone wrapped in bacon and dipped in peanut butter.

"That doesn't make any sense." Carissa didn't want to admit it aloud, but Jacqueline was the obvious choice for first up on the show. After all, that was the big start. The introduction episode that dove into an in-depth hour-long special about a specific business, the owner, and how it was the heart of the town. The one that launched mini-segments with only highlights of the other town stores in twenty-minutes or less. "You'd think they'd want to start with something more exciting and trending than a bakery."

"Wait, you said bakers. As in plural," Felicia said.

"Why yes… Remember, this is a competition. Renee Wilson and her girls are all competing, remember?" Ms. Horton strutted to the window as if to add tension to her words. "I'm sure that I can arrange for Tabitha to meet with Drew Lancaster first. Maybe you won't even have to be bothered if she wins him over."

Ms. Horton threw down the preschool anti-pretentious pact. The only thing that would reunite the Fabulous Five against a common enemy. Based on the sour expressions on the other faces in the room, Carissa wasn't the only one who had caught on.

"Pulling out that card, are we?" Jackie asked, more of a rhetorical statement than an actual question.

"We need to convince him to start with someone else besides me." Carissa shot Stella a pleading stare.

"Drew Lancaster insisted that we start with a bakery." Ms. Horton picked up a pen, the gold one that all of the girls had chipped in for before they graduated high school. It was a promise to her that they would always remember what she'd taught them.

"Drew Lancaster? His name even sounds like a pompous jerk."

7

Stella grunted for extra emphasis. "If we can't meet for five minutes, then how can we work together for five months?"

"Listen, I realize these corporate types need to be treated as if they're everything in the world, so don't worry about it. I'll just send him to Tabitha," Ms. Horton said in a matter-of-fact tone.

"Like a toddler still on a pacifier," Stella muttered under her breath.

She protested too much, which meant she needed this more than she would admit. They all knew her business was struggling the most in recent years. And even after all this time, as much as Carissa held so much resentment toward Jackie, she still couldn't let the rest of her childhood friends lose to their arch enemies. No way would she allow them to win this program. Maybe if she spoke to this exec, she could convince him to start with one of the other girls first...another of the Fabulous Five. "Fine, I'll meet with the glorified party planner." Carissa realized that Jackie had a point. She did sound more like Stella than herself today. Good, maybe it was time for Carissa to give up her sweet-doormat title. It was time to take a walk and cool off before she met with this Drew character, so she turned on her heels and smacked into something hard and large. She rubbed her nose free of sting and blinked up at a perfect stranger. Perfect height, perfect hair, perfect lips.

"You okay there?" His deep voice closed in around her.

Space. That's what she needed. She moved away and took a breath. A breath of Ode de Mysterious with an undertone of trouble. After a moment, she managed to turn her January gloom into a friendly welcome. "Yes, I am now. Thank you. Sorry. Who are you?"

He quirked an attitude-changing grin at her. "I'm the pompous, glorified party planner, toddler, stuck-on-a-pacifier Drew Lancaster."

CHAPTER TWO

THE SMALL-FRAMED WOMAN with wild blonde hair took a step away from Drew. She had an unassuming attractiveness, a quiet, understated natural beauty, but the misbuttoned shirt and scuffed boots made her look unkempt.

She stumbled away two more steps and blinked. Her long lashes accentuated her light eyes above her round, rosy cheeks.

The room was silent. He usually enjoyed having the upper hand. Not in this case. Not when the words of his aunt Sally echoed through his head about women. *One or two is a pleasant conversation. Three or more are a gaggle of trouble.* And in this case, there were six ladies in one room, all with stares that would frighten his Silver Star–recipient commanding officer in Iraq.

He straightened his tie and lifted his chin but kept his back to the doorway. Always leave an escape route open in all types of battles. The sweet perfume infiltrating his senses from the red-haired model distracted him, although not in a good way. She frightened him. He rubbed the back of his head, remembering how Knox's ex took him out with a garden gnome. Women like this were trouble.

"We're so glad you're here, Mr. Lancaster. Right, ladies?" The woman he assumed to be Mayor Horton—considering her professional dress, age, and position in the room behind the desk —said.

The model woman with bright red hair sauntered toward him. Yep, she would definitely be his boss and former comrade's type. For half a second, he swore snakes were going to slither around her beautiful face and turn him to stone. Those green eyes were piercing. "Yes, I for one am excited to make your acquaintance. I'm Jacqueline Ramor," she said in a slithery tone.

"I for one…please. Get over yourself. Listen, I'm Stella, the girl who fixes cars. If Knox man ever shows up, let him know I can fix anything with an engine. Until then, I'm out." The woman with dark hair and a Latino accent brushed past Drew without even a sideways glance.

"You'll have to excuse Stella. She's had a rough day," Mayor Horton said.

"You mean rough life," Jacqueline muttered from the edge of his peripheral vision.

Before he had a chance to catch his breath with the whirl of women around him, another one approached. "I'm Felicia." She inserted herself between him and the door, cutting off his escape route. He was surrounded.

She was an interesting beauty, a mix of dark features with pale skin. "I run the local plant nursery. If you need any flowers for your project, I'm the girl to see." She shook his hand and didn't let go, not until the woman he'd run into on the way inside took her by the shoulders and led her to the corner of the room.

"Relax. There's no camera on yet." Jacqueline slid her purse up her arm with the dignity of a starlet.

A taller woman with a hefty amount of jewelry and a long neck approached. "I'm Mary-Beth. I'm sure you'll be stopping by Maple Grounds, my coffee shop, while you're here. We have beans from around the world, but we specialize in our own sugar maple blend here."

"I need a caffeine fix soon, I assure you. For now, I need my room and to line up meetings with the bakers."

"That would be me. I'm Carissa Donahue, the owner and pastry chef of Sugar and Soul Bakery."

Finally, a name for the unassuming female who'd knocked into him. She brushed the unruly frizz away from her face. If she tied her hair back in a neat bun, she'd be stunning, with those high cheek bones and slender yet curvy frame.

"Guess we should go chat," Carissa said with a pop of her hip.

"Go chat?" He glanced around, realizing he was alone in this. Not good. His assistant, that's what he needed. "Lori, my assistant, will call to schedule a meeting. I only stopped by the mayor's office to get a key for our meeting rooms." Meeting rooms he needed to get this stunt of a project moving forward before it was too late. The only project to save Knox from ruin, himself from ruin, and a small town from ruin.

No pressure.

Or better yet, one of the scouts Knox had sent to Georgia and Alabama would discover a better town to work with and he'd be off the hook without refusing to bow to Knox's whim. He owed the man his respect, a comrade in arms and a childhood friend, but this man wasn't the same one he once knew. This man was living life on the edge without a plan. He had to be if he'd sent his number one to Nowhere, USA.

"Oh, darn. I'm so sorry about that." Mayor Horton waved a hand in front of her face as if it were ninety degrees instead of nineteen outside. "I'd meant to leave all of this at the inn for you, but since you're here, you can meet some of the business owners in our town. What a happy circumstance."

Circumstance implied there wasn't manipulation utilized to get him here. Lori had already told the mayor he didn't have time today to meet. That she'd have to make an appointment in a few days. Enough with the games. He'd written the manual on how to manipulate to get the job done. Cordial undertones and persuasive smiles weren't working, and he needed to expediate things. "I don't have time for power struggles in this project. You need this production, so work with me. I'm the last man standing. The only one willing to give this a chance, so let's start working together."

The mayor didn't acknowledge his statement. Instead, she rounded her desk. "I'm afraid there was a flood in our main building that we utilized for our recreation center and conference rooms. Don't worry, though. I have the perfect space for you to work. There's plenty of room for corporate meetings, and it'll give you a chance to meet more of the people of Sugar Maple, since the recreation center is below the offices. It's a lovely space and even has a place to sleep as you requested. Although, I'm sure you'd rather sleep in the lovely inn."

Carissa shot forward. "But that's—"

"And it hasn't been used in a long time. I think it's time to move on. We all want to show Mr. Drew Lancaster our southern hospitality, right?" The mayor offered a placating smile to Carissa.

He didn't know what kind of power this mayor had over these women, but they snapped to her will. "Right, so we're all set."

The mayor opened a drawer at her desk and then handed him a key with a large pacifier keychain and a spiral-bound notebook. "Here is a sort of introduction for your stay, including various directions for the area, information for your offices, local business names, and prominent members of the community you might want to speak with." She thrust the notebook to his chest. "Carissa can show you the way. Enjoy our town, Mr. Lancaster, and please don't hesitate to let any of us know what you need. We'd be happy to provide it for you."

He took the key and slipped it into his pocket. "No need for the escort. Despite popular belief, I'm not a child who needs to be coddled." Before the gaggle of women had the opportunity to gang up on him, he left the mayor's office and returned to the salt-covered sidewalk outside the prehistoric courthouse building.

His dress shoes were no match for the slick surface, so he had to shuffle along, using his abs to keep from falling back and hitting his head. Maybe that would be a good thing. What was he thinking, coming to this remote town in the Tennessee mountains? He knew why, but he didn't like it.

"If Knox had listened to me in the first place..." he grumbled with each step he took along the dead tree–lined square.

"Not everyone can control their heart the way you can." Lori's words cut through him like the icy wind through his thin coat.

He spun on his heels, but he couldn't stop and ended up doing a 280 before grabbing a tree to stop himself. "Get me out of here," he ground out.

She chuckled. "Let me guess... You already assessed everyone you've met and deduced this is a waste of your time."

He straightened himself to his full six-foot-three frame. "Come on. You and I both know I don't deserve this."

"Tell me, how did the initial meeting go? Did you make friends and set up a rapport so we could work well with the residents here?" Lori walked in her snow boots past him, executed a perfect turn to face him, and crossed her arms over her chest. "Or did you try to control everything until you alienated the room?"

He shuffled to the next building and grabbed hold of a wrought iron railing at the bottom of a boarded-up storefront. Yep, this town needed him more than he needed them. "I dazzled them."

"Good boy." She patted him on the shoulder, causing him to play happy feet with the ground.

When he finally managed to settle and catch his breath, he asked, "What's the good news? Tell me that one of the other towns got a green light."

"The town in Georgia is out of the running for this project.

The grandma they were spotlighting is accused of scraping off 'made in China' and calling her merchandise antiques."

"Are all small-town folk crazy?" He rubbed the scar on the back of his head. "Okay, so that means it's between this town and one other now? Good. I still have a chance to escape."

"Nope." Lori tugged her bright-blue hat over her ears.

"No? I thought they were finalizing these last three."

"They did. You're it. This is your chance to redeem yourself in Knox's eyes."

"Me, redeem myself?" Agitation warmed his skin, but not enough in the icy air. "If Knox would stop making his decisions based on hunches and feelings, then we wouldn't be in this mess."

"Cut him some slack. He's human and has a heart like a real man." Lori tilted her head to the side the way she did when she wanted him to understand her subtext.

He decided to redirect the conversation. "That's good news, huh?" He tried to sound pleased, but the more he held tight to remain standing, the more he felt himself slipping away from the life he once lived.

"You have no idea. Listen, Knox changed his mind and chose someone else to go in your place. That's why I rushed us out here. I already confirmed our arrival and that you've met with the mayor to kick things off."

"Why didn't he want me on this project? I'm the best man he's got. The man who served with him, watched each other's backs for two years. We're friends."

"You're efficient, organized, top dog when it comes to executing any plan."

"You say that as if it's a bad thing." He caught sight of Carissa exiting the courthouse and trudging across the square to a little storefront with Sugar and Soul Bakery written on the front. That's when he realized he'd made it to the end of his slippery road. One more building down had to be the offices, so he shuffled forward.

"No. But for this project he wanted someone more…soft handed and friendly. "

"I can be friendly." He offered his best political smile.

She laughed. "You look like Knox when he got caught in the middle of the consumer backlash after the automotive fiasco."

"Harsh. But that proves my point. If he hadn't been distracted by his romantic entanglements in the tabloids, he would not have endorsed a business that stole from the elderly."

Lori hoisted him up the first step, and he grabbed hold of the railing before thrusting his hand in his pocket to dig out the key. "More the reason that Knox needs you even if he doesn't realize it. It's our job to make the world believe in him again. As you said, you two always had each other's backs. He gave you this job when you first got out, despite your lack of experience. Just show the warm side of Knox and how he relates to people."

"So, lie to the world by manipulating these people? Great plan."

He dropped the pacifier keychain into Lori's red knit mittens.

She glanced down at the keychain. "Cute. I guess we know where our starting line is in this project." She shook her head and slid the key into the door. "Speaking of romantic entanglements… Are you ever going to give a relationship a real try? I mean beyond the work functions that require a plus one?"

"I date. I had a girlfriend last year. We dated for a month. She cried when I told her that our schedules didn't correlate well. It was messy."

"Sometimes life's messy."

"No time to head shrink me. We have work to do. Besides, she was an accountant. They are supposed to appreciate facts."

"Yeah, probably not the fact that you didn't think she was worth marrying." She held up her hands before he had a chance to defend himself. "All I'm saying is that you know Knox blames you for ending his relationship and causing a scene that damaged his career."

Drew opened his mouth to protest, but she held one finger up at him. "It doesn't matter what really happened. Knox is the man who has the power, and you don't want to be fired by Knox Brevard. Despite his recent public image issues, he still can make a phone call and blacklist you."

"That's illegal."

She shrugged. "In indie Hollywood, who's going to enforce that? You finish this out and make it work, and you can write your ticket to the big screen. And as for your head shrinking, I'm not paid enough."

He leaned against the railing, tired from the last few exhausting weeks of scrambling to keep his job. "If we could just keep women away from Knox, maybe we'd have a shot here. Women are trouble."

"Hey," she huffed.

"I didn't mean you."

"Why? Because I'm not dating material?"

"I…I mean—"

"Relax. I'm just showing you how your ex might have felt. As a matter of fact, you're one to talk. You've got an overcrowded train of exes you've left in your wake. You better find a way to open your heart and let a nice woman into your life before one of those exes ties you to a track and drives over you." She turned the key and pushed on the door, but it didn't open.

"Cute." He nudged her out of the way and threw his body weight into the door, which flew open and sent him several steps into a dark hallway.

"Glad you noticed."

Drew shifted between feet. "Ah, Lori. You work with me. Didn't we just say—"

"Relax. Tall, dark, and damaged isn't my type." Lori shut the door behind her and removed her gloves. "I'm going to do you a favor. I'm going to pick out your next girlfriend. Not the corporate business transaction kind of date that you're used to.

Someone who'll turn you inside out and around until you're dizzy."

Images of his childhood sweetheart turned runaway bride sent a shiver through him. "No thanks. Besides, no woman has the power to do that to me. Just get me through this job."

Lori's laughter echoed through the hallway, up the stairs, and into his heart. She was the one woman he could always count on. A true friend. "I didn't take Drew Lancaster for being someone afraid to take on a challenge."

He flicked on the lights and let out a long, white-cloud breath. "I'm not scared of anything."

"Then prove it." Lori bit her bottom lip at the edge, something she did when she was devising a devious plan. "I pick a woman, and you have to go out with her. If after two weeks of dating, you don't fall for her, then you win, and I never mention your personal life again."

He rubbed his arms to keep warm. "And if I win?"

"Then I'll call in a favor with my father and get us a job on his Hollywood set. I know how you've wanted to return to California since you started this job with Knox."

His muscles relaxed at the thought of going to his childhood home. His aunt's house had been left on that beautiful piece of property. No, that was the past, not the future. "You said you'd never use that connection, even if you were starving and living on the streets with rats."

"That's how sure I am that I'm going to win." Lori removed her mitten and held out her hand.

He took it. "Fine, but this is a sucker bet. I almost feel bad for you. That being said, if this gets me into a real job far from Knox Brevard, I'm in. I love the man as a brother, but he's too...unpredictable to work for."

"We'll work out the details while we set up in here. First thing, you need to head to the inn and change into something warmer and more practical. If you had waited two minutes, you could've gone with me to the inn before mowing over everyone to start working."

He swished his lips, keeping his aggravation to himself.

"I know. I know. Working efficiently is more important than comfort. Please tell me you brought something with you besides Italian dress shoes, leather jacket, and suit pants, though."

He shook his head. For the first time, the realization of his situation sank in, and he didn't like the feeling of being out of control.

"Don't worry. I packed an extra bag for you. It's in the car. And Drew?"

"Yes?"

Lori set her purse onto a side table. "You better marry yourself to this idea, because when I win, you'll need to turn Knox's career around if you hope to get a job higher up on the food chain."

His face flushed; his heart raced. Marry? Why would she use that word? He opened the door and stepped into the cold, realizing she had a point. For the first time since his military days, Drew Lancaster needed to commit to something. The only problem was that commitment made him want to go on a two-hundred-mile run in his dress shoes on ice.

CHAPTER THREE

"WHAT'S GOING on in here? It's like a flour eruption!" Ms. Horton tossed her briefcase onto the wooden island in the heart of the bakery kitchen and twirled Carissa about. "Oh dear. Have you slept at all?"

Carissa's head felt like a pressure cooker ready to explode. How could the entire town economy rest on her shoulders alone? "Look. I made all of this for the tasting. All the town favorites. I'm sure to win this contest and secure this deal, right? I mean, my tarts and pies and cookies are the best."

"Calm down. Sit." Ms. Horton pushed her onto the stepladder and dusted her cheeks. "Yes, I'm sure all this is great, but Mr. Lancaster already finished up with Tabitha and he's on his way here."

Carissa shot out of the stool. If he was on his way, she needed to decorate the cupcakes. "I've never worked so hard for something I didn't want before." She held the frosting tube too tight, and it squirted white goo all over her hand.

"Put down the frosting and step away from the counter," Ms. Horton ordered.

"What? Did Tabitha already win?" She sighed and tossed the

frosting tube onto the counter. "I don't know if I'm upset or relieved."

"No. She hasn't won." Ms. Horton grabbed a hand towel, dipped it under the faucet, looked at Carissa's face, and then backed away with a shake of her head. "I need reinforcements."

Carissa closed her eyes. The hot kitchen was suffocating her. How many hours had she been working? Her neck ache told her all night, her hands felt the hours of kneading dough, but her nerves were raw and aware.

Ms. Horton retrieved her phone from her purse.

"What are you doing?"

"Calling the girls." Ms. Horton typed away on her phone and then grabbed an apron. "You stay. Don't move." She whizzed around the kitchen, wiping down the counters and tossing dishes into the sink.

Carissa sat there with energy draining from her. "Why, if Tabitha already won?"

Ms. Horton didn't say anything or even look up from a texting frenzy.

The bell at the front of her store jingled.

"I thought I put the closed sign out front."

"You did." Stella walked into the Kitchen, thick leather jacket already sliding down her arms. She tossed it on a chair and headed toward the stove.

Felicia stopped at the edge, her normal neutral expression morphed to shock and disgust. "Dear Lord, this is worse than you said." She looked to Stella. "Truce for one hour?"

Stella gave a sharp nod. "Let's get you upstairs."

"Why? What's going on? I thought Tabitha won."

"No, dear. She blew it. When Mr. Lancaster showed up, Tabitha had burned the cookies and set fire to a towel. They had to call the fire department. Mary-Beth is stalling him at her coffee shop to give us time."

"This is on you." Stella crossed the room and lifted Carissa up by the shoulders. "Based on the smell in this place, you're gonna wow them, sister."

"Then it really is all on me," Carissa mumbled, the weight of the truth resting like a forty-pound, century-old fruit cake on her shoulders.

Stella offered her best attempt at a friendly smile. She looked constipated. "What is?"

Carissa blinked away the sting of no sleep. "The town. If I don't wow them, then this could be the end of the road for the entire show. Which is what I want, but not what is best." She rubbed her temple, trying to get rid of the conundrum pounding at her skull.

Ms. Horton waved Felicia to the sink. "Work on those dishes. Stella, you get that girl upstairs and find her a change of clothes. We need all hands on deck here, ladies."

The door chimed again, and they all froze. Mary-Beth entered with her crazy container of makeup and jewelry supplies.

"Whoa, good thing I'm here." Mary-Beth rushed into the kitchen, crossing a proverbial line by entering the bakery. She stopped at the edge of the stove. "Thought we called a truce."

Stella waved her hands to get Carissa's attention. "I know this is asking a lot, but the truce holds until sundown, got it?"

Carissa nodded, unable to say the words. But there were a few she had to ask. "What about Jud...I mean Jackie?"

Mary-Beth snatched Carissa by the elbow and led her to the stairs. "I thought it best that she kept Mr. Lancaster company while we worked together here."

"Good thinking," Ms. Horton said. "I really miss this. The teamwork, I mean."

They all ignored Ms. Horton's attempt at untwining the barbed wire fence.

"Come on, girl. We've got some work to do. Good thing I brought the concealer. You look like you haven't slept in ten days."

"Try ten years," Carissa mumbled under her breath but followed Mary-Beth, who ignored Carissa's quiet dig and pushed her into the bathroom. "Shower and wash your hair. I'll go pick out a dress."

Carissa fought past the anger and the exhaustion and did what needed to be done. She couldn't let everyone down. And she knew that Mary-Beth was the best chance at making her look presentable. The girl had always had a gift at working makeover miracles. A flash of the prom-saving makeover made her laugh. Only Mary-Beth could fix a fall-down-the-stairs-dress-ripping-hair-disheveled-makeup smear into a Runway Cinderella look.

The aroma of her favorite pumpkin and maple cookies were replaced by floral shampoo and soap.

"Hurry up in there. No time to waste. Jackie texted. She's having trouble keeping him there."

Jackie. Such a familiar name for such a foreign friend. "I guess not every man will fall for her charms." Carissa shut off the water, dried, and wrapped a towel around herself and then opened the bathroom door to face her fate.

Mary-Beth took Carissa by the shoulders. "I know you still hate her and me, but we're going to ignore that for now."

A slap of realization stung her insides. "I don't hate you." Carissa fidgeted with the edge of her towel. "It's just that I can't be around you when she's there."

Mary-Beth turned her leaf earrings between her fingers twice before she popped back into action. "Here, sit. I'll dry your hair and apply makeup." She ran a comb through Carissa's long hair. "Thank you."

"For what?"

"For not hating me. I hate myself sometimes." She turned on the blow dryer before Carissa had a chance to ask why.

Halfway through blow drying Carissa's hair Mary-Beth checked her phone again. "Out of time. Project Jackie failed.

Here, put this on." A dress with a silver bodice and sage bottom was tossed in Carissa's lap.

"Isn't this a little much? I'm supposed to be baking, not modeling. I'm not Jackie. I won't win this guy over with looks."

At least the shower had provided some energy and woke Carissa up enough to remember to put on a bra before she slid the dress over her head. Shoes were shoved onto her feet, and she was nudged back into the chair. "No time to finish drying, so a quick updo it is."

Within two minutes, Carissa's hair was in a neat bun on top of her head, and Mary-Beth turned her around with lipstick in hand.

Carissa preferred natural, no-fuss kind of wear, but she knew better than to argue until Mary-Beth went at her with an over-sized cherry blossom earring. "Nope, no way." She held up a hand.

"Just wanted to see if you were awake." Mary-Beth winked and then handed her two studs with sage and silver flowers.

"What were you saying about not being pretty enough to win over Mr. Lancaster? I think he's going to fall flat at your feet when he sees you like this. Dang, girl, you're hot." Mary-Beth's southern drawl made her words sound more legit, but Carissa never wanted to be the hottest girl in town. Just hot enough to keep a man from Jackie.

She spun Carissa to face herself in the mirror. Who was that girl? "I forgot how good you were with friend makeovers. The last one you did for me you helped me get ready for..." Her words had gotten ahead of her brain.

"The proposal dinner." Mary-Beth's eyes watered, and she sniffled. "I'm sorry. I know."

Flashes of no ring, only her all-but-ring-on-finger fiancé's exit from the restaurant with her best friend threatened to send her back to bed. A place she avoided except when extreme exhaustion took hold, since it was the loneliest spot in her apartment. "What did you mean about hating yourself?" Carissa stood and faced one of her oldest and dearest friends she'd barely spoken to in a decade, and that's when she saw it. The pain in Mary-Beth's eyes that she'd felt in her heart.

"Girls, he's here. Hurry up!" Ms. Horton shouted up the stairs.

Mary-Beth smoothed a wayward hair back from Carissa's face. "Let's go. You're ready."

She didn't feel ready, but she shuffled down the stairs, following Mary-Beth, and managed to reach the kitchen before the front door chimed.

"At least it smells better in here." The deep voice of Mr. Lancaster echoed from the storefront.

Stella whistled like a construction worker at Carissa. "Didn't know you were gonna win the show that way. You go, girl."

Felicia nodded. "You look nice. You've got this."

Ms. Horton opened the curtain between the kitchen and storefront and whispered, "You look lovely, darling, and your baked goods smell amazing."

"Thank you." Carissa stepped out into the bake shop and stopped behind the display case, where the girls and Ms. Horton had obviously finished setting all the baked goods out.

"Wow," Mr. Lancaster said, looking straight at Carissa.

The way he looked at her almost made her think he was commenting about how she looked instead of about the scones and cupcakes and tarts. All the words of affirmation flung at her from her friends had messed with her crazy brain. "Thanks. I worked hard on everything." She moved closer to the display case and wished she knew which item would be the best to start with, but it might be the only one he tried. If it wasn't good, he'd call this off. Which would be great in her book, but not good for the town.

The woman next to him elbowed him in the side. "Hi, I'm Lori Brewster, Mr. Lancaster's assistant."

"Nice to meet you." Carissa stood there not moving. Dang it, she should've offered her hand. This was business. Jackie appeared behind them, and all senses vacated Carissa's brain. All thought was sucked into the pit of betrayal instead of the plan for the future.

Jackie sauntered to the case. "If you like the aroma, you'll like the taste even better. Our little small-town girl here was meant to be in the kitchen."

Carissa knew Jackie meant it as an insult, but she was too tired to care.

Mary-Beth shot forward and took Jackie by the elbow. "So, let's allow them time to taste it. We need to head back to my coffee shop. See y'all later."

Perhaps it was exhaustion, but there was no way Carissa could hold a grudge against Mary-Beth any longer. She didn't decide to steal the man Carissa loved; she just didn't want to hate anyone. That's when Carissa realized it was time to let go of the past and think about the future. This was her shot to do something real with her life. To make a difference in the town she loved.

"The smell of cinnamon and sugar doesn't sell a product on television." Mr. Lancaster straightened his tie, the way he had when entering Ms. Horton's office yesterday. Carissa wanted to snug that tie up tight around his smug expression.

"Smell is part of the tasting experience." Carissa broke through the blockade of emotions crippling her and removed a pumpkin and maple cookie from the case. "That being said, I assure you that it tastes even better."

"Taste doesn't translate to television either. It's all about visual presentation." He marched forward, looked down his nose at the case, and then shook his head. "This is plain, hum-drum, no life to it. This won't sell anything, certainly not Knox Brevard's fans. They have distinguished tastes."

Lori joined him. "If you mean buying blow-up poop emojis as Christmas gifts distinguished."

Carissa didn't know Lori, but at that moment, she wanted to get to know her more than Mr. Lancaster.

"That's something we can work on, maybe hire one of our own pastry chefs to help put a sprinkle of pizzazz on these obviously tasty items."

"Then it wouldn't be my creation, would it?" Carissa opened the case again, retrieved one of her tarts, and placed it on the top of the case with two spoons. "Take a taste before you judge my work."

Lori lifted a spoon, but Mr. Lancaster took a step away. "I don't eat sugar. As I said, Ms. Donahue, the items must be visually appealing."

"Excuse us for a moment, please," his assistant said before ushering him to the corner and whispering something to him. Her brows were furrowed, and she had a firm grip on his arm.

Carissa looked to her remaining friends, but they only shrugged, and Ms. Horton stood with her typical analytical gaze.

Mr. Lancaster argued something, but in the end, he swiveled to face Ms. Horton. "My assistant has graciously offered to provide some guidance on this project. You, Ms. Horton, need to make sure that your baker is willing to make some adjustments. She might know baking, but I know television."

Without another word, he blew out the door like a frosty wind gust with his assistant following behind him.

Stella slammed her palm down on the counter. "I dare him to speak to you that way. This isn't going to work. He needs to go."

"As much as I hate to admit it, why couldn't they start with the fashion segment of the town? Jackie's much better at this than I am. She can win any man over."

Ms. Horton crossed the kitchen and placed a motherly hand on Carissa's shoulder. "Trust me when I say that you are the only one right now who can do this. It was my choice to start with the baking segment because I know you're our best chance. You're sweet, kind, and determined. It's time for some tough love here."

She cleared her throat and glanced at Stella, as if to warn her what she was about to say she might not like but that she should keep her big mouth shut.

Carissa straightened and looked up, ready to face whatever it was that Ms. Horton would throw at her. "Jackie doesn't have the power to steal this away from you. Just like she didn't have the power to steal Mark from you. You two weren't meant to be together. You wanted it to work out because your parents had left, you were graduating high school, and you didn't know what you wanted to do with your life. You were scared, and that's why you wanted Mark in your life. I believe that Jackie did you a favor."

"That's going too far." Stella closed in, but Ms. Horton held one hand up.

"Do you know what Mark is doing now?" Ms. Horton asked.

Carissa shook her head. "No. Last I heard, Jackie dumped him eight months after they left."

"No, he dumped her. He tried to get back with her, but she said no. He's unemployed and living with his father in Texas."

"How do you know that?" Carissa asked.

"Because he wanted to come back to Sugar Maple to work. His application came across my desk."

Carissa's pulse clicked away like a timer on hyper speed.

"Don't worry. His application was rejected. That isn't the point. The point is that you were too good for him. If you two had married, you wouldn't be who you are today. You're a strong, independent, beautiful, and talented woman who created her dream job, despite having no family here, or resources, or a husband. You earned this job, and I believe you'll earn this contract."

Ms. Horton's words of encouragement touched her heart, and she logically knew some of it was true, but self-esteem played cruel jokes at times. She wanted to be confident and feel good about her accomplishments, but in actuality she wanted to do more. She'd been holding herself back, afraid she'd push too far for her dreams and she'd lose everything. "Jackie's right. I belong in the kitchen. Someone else will always need to dress me up to be worthy of people like Mr. Lancaster. I won't give up, but we all know what Mr. Lancaster is saying is the truth. TV doesn't care about smells and tastes or even how kind a person is. It is all about appearance. I can cook and bake and provide delicious treats, but someone will always have to dress up my food, just like people have to dress me up. I'm simple, and I don't belong in the world of television."

CHAPTER FOUR

DREW SHUFFLED FROM THE BAKERY, admitting to himself that Lori had saved him from a concussion with the boots she'd packed for him. She was right about that and everything else about him. Except this project. His gut was all twisted. It had to be a sign to end this ridiculous project. He hadn't felt like this since he was in Iraq.

"What are you doing? We already talked about this; you need this to work." Lori snuggled her scarf around her neck. Was she as cold as he was? He needed to get the heat working in those darn offices better.

He halted and pointed to the quaint bakery building with a brick front, orange awning, and wrought iron touches. "You saw those desserts. They were plain. They won't translate to viewers."

"Then why'd you say wow when we walked in and you looked —wait a minute." She halted mid-step, placed her foot down, and tapped her lips. "You were talking about her, not the desserts. It was the girl, not the food who got you all twisted up."

"Don't be ridiculous. I saw right through Jacqueline Ramor the moment I met her. Trust me. You've got nothing to worry about." Drew walked around Lori and headed across the town center toward their very-temporary offices. "She's a Knox girl. Not for me at all."

"Not Jackie. Carissa. Your eyes nearly popped out of your head when she walked out."

"Carissa?" Drew snorted at the absurdity. "She's not my type. Do you know when I saw her yesterday, she had flour on her hands? She didn't even have her shirt buttoned correctly."

"And OCD Drew noticed these things. That's why you said wow. She caught you off guard. Mr. I-got-women-pegged was shocked by an unexpected change, and that broke the perfect façade of Drew Lancaster. I've never seen you thrown off like that before. Oh, I think I've found the girl for you!"

He pulled the key from his pocket and opened the door to the building they'd be stuck working in for days, rushing inside out of the winter air and Lori's questions. "You're insane."

"Stop running." Lori shut the door behind her, but she only tightened her scarf around her neck and didn't remove her coat. Not that he did, either.

Dang, it was cold in this place. "I'm not running away from you. I have work." He trudged up the stairs and tucked his chin into his coat. What happened to heat rising?

"Not from me, from Carissa. She scared you, didn't she?" Lori wrapped her arms around herself and shivered in the corner.

He lowered to the desk chair and retrieved his laptop from his bag. "This mountain town is getting to you. You must be getting altitude sickness."

"At around five thousand feet? I don't think so. I grew up in 15,000 feet in the Rocky Mountains."

"You grew up in the Rockies?" Drew rubbed his forehead, trying to jar that memory.

"Yes, but you shouldn't know that because you don't need to know that for the job." Lori stared at him with her I-rest-my-case expression.

This was the awkward moment where they had to bond or

something. Drew opened his laptop and typed in his code. "You make it sound like all I care about is work. That I don't have time for a personal life." Personal lives were overrated.

"That's why any time I ask you a question about your dating life, you open that laptop." Lori flopped down in a chair near him and crossed her foot over her other ankle. That meant she'd be staying until she decided the conversation was over. If she wasn't so good at her job, he wouldn't tolerate such distractions.

"You're exaggerating." He blew warm air over his hands, trying to get his fingers to thaw enough to type.

"Really? The minute I mentioned your personal life, you ran for your laptop." She held a red-mittened hand toward his computer.

She had a point. He didn't have to admit it, though. "Since you're not going to let this go, talk." He swiveled to face her.

"Tell me what happened with the last woman. All I know is you decided your schedules didn't work. That isn't a reason."

Drew threw his hands up, rotated in his chair, and kicked the radiator, but there was no response. "We dated for a few months. She's in finance. We communicated mostly via text and email, and we dated on a schedule to avoid having to cancel and reschedule."

"She sounds perfect. Schedules, spreadsheets, stone-cold communication, oh my." Lori removed her gloves and moved to the radiator beside him.

"Yes, well, it wasn't, so we ended it." He shot up from the computer. Enough was enough. He didn't need to work under these extreme conditions. They needed to give them offices with heat.

Lori cut off his path to the doorway. "Nope. Not getting off that easy. Why didn't it work out? Did she schedule a date on the wrong day? Did she forget to wear matching earrings?"

Irritation nipped at his temper, but he refused to let her get a rise out of him. It would only prove her point. "You think you know me so well. No, that wasn't why."

"Then why?"

"She ended things when I was thirty minutes late one day," he huffed.

"Why were you late?" Lori asked, as if referencing a normal day.

"You know why. I was at the hospital with Knox after his girlfriend went crazy. *That man* needs your help picking a woman. Go bother him."

Lori followed him down the stairs and out the front door. "You just wait. You'll fall in love someday, and you'll understand why a man can make a fool out of himself over a woman."

"I'll never get hit over the head with a garden gnome. And I will never make a fool out of myself over some woman." He marched down the street and up past the receptionist for the county offices, up the stairs, and into the mayor's office. "Do you realize that Knox Brevard is doing you a favor by choosing your town for this segment? You should be rolling out the red carpet for us. Instead you have our offices nowhere near our accommodations, I've been almost set on fire by one baker, and I was grossly disappointed with the product of another. Now I return to the offices to discover the heating doesn't work. If you don't want us here, we can leave now."

Ms. Horton rose from her chair behind her desk with a school principal expression. "First, Mr. Lancaster, we did roll out our welcome mat to you. I'm sorry that it doesn't meet your city expectations. As for the mishap earlier, the towel caught fire, not you. And if you had tasted Carissa's amazing product, you would've been able to do your job better. Perhaps if you knew what it tasted like, you could give her pointers on how to present it."

His agitation didn't waver. The woman was playing some sort of small-town games with him, and he wouldn't stand for it. "We need offices with heat in this cold. If not, I can assure you we will be leaving."

"I guess if that is Knox Brevard's wish, we cannot stop you." Mayor Horton turned her computer screen around to show Knox with a sour, deep-grooved forehead staring him down. She headed for the door. "I'll let you two speak about your plans, and you can let me know what you decide. Oh, but if you do decide to stay, you might want to turn the heater on. The valve is on the side of the radiator, and the directions are in the packet of information I presented you when you arrived."

Drew ran a hand through his hair. He'd forgotten about that silly manual. The door shut, and Knox cleared his throat on the video chat. "This is your idea of selling me and my brand to this town? Didn't you say I needed this if I wanted to restore my good name after Samantha lied to the media and made me look like a womanizing monster?"

Now wasn't the time for Drew to point out that Samantha had a point. Instead he swallowed his pride, yet again, for a man he owed his life to and his future. "It was a misunderstanding. I'll smooth things over. Don't worry about it."

"I hope I don't have to come to that town to do your job. The one I hired you to do when you had no other employment opportunities when you returned to the States. It's been five years now; I shouldn't have to hold your hand to keep your temper from getting you in trouble anymore."

"I don't have a temper." Drew lifted his chin. It had been five years of him working on cleaning up Knox's messes and less about his actual job.

The door creaked behind him.

"I'll keep you posted on how things are going." Drew wanted to click end for the video conference, but since Knox had been on with the mayor, he let it be. If only he could break free of Knox and his controlling ways, then he wouldn't be frustrated all the time. Sure, he'd had a temper and a mouth on him when he'd left the military, but now he could be polite and as smooth talking as Knox any day.

He turned to see Ms. Horton at the door tapping her foot. "Everything worked out?"

Drew didn't like it when someone controlled the situation. Not at all. "Of course."

Ms. Horton opened her door wider. "That's good news, because the town elders are waiting for you in your office. They are the ones you still need to win over."

"Win over? What are you talking about?" Drew fisted his hands and shoved them into his pocket before Knox could see his anger boiling to the surface. "I thought you were the mayor of this town." There... He knew a woman who held such a prestigious position had to be into the power.

"That's right, I'm the mayor, but I'm far from the one who runs this town. I answer to the town elders. If I were you, I'd get moving. They don't like it when people are late. They are old school."

"What are you doing still standing there? Move it, soldier," Knox commanded as if he were his commanding officer.

He swallowed the agitation and put on a fresh smile. "I will win over the esteemed elder committee with no issue. I can deal with professional, mature people."

"Right. I'm sure you can." Mayor Horton approached the desk, turned her screen around to face away from him, and sat down.

"Is he still standing there? If so, tell him to drop and give you fifty."

Drew right faced and marched out of the room before he could say how he really felt. This was it, the last project he'd work on for Knox. He needed as far away from his womanizing, crazy ways as he could get.

WHY WAS January the unofficial Everyone Diet month? It had been three hours since a customer entered, an hour since Carissa took a cat nap, and thirty minutes since she stopped scrubbing everything clean.

The aroma of cinnamon, pumpkin, and baked crusts was bittersweet. Enough. She wasn't going to let her hard work go to waste. If no one came by today, she'd take some to those who'd appreciate it. Her favorite sweet tooth locals.

She packaged up all the leftover baked goods, flipped the sign over to Closed, put on her winter coat, and marched across the town square. The sleet stuck to the brown grass and sidewalk, making it slick. The cold froze the end of her nose and ears, so she trudged faster. Not that she was in a hurry to enter the building Mark used to live in, but Ms. Horton was right. It was time to move on.

Three parking spaces were taken up by the white minibus. Good, they were there right on time. It was convenient that the recreation center was under construction and the elders had to meet in the old abandoned storefront. Ms. Horton probably planned it so the square would be a little less empty when the Knox show people arrived.

Carissa entered, set her boxes on the entryway table, and removed her coat and hat. The sound of the commotion lightened her heart. Some people saw therapists, others talked to friends, but when life was tough, Carissa would bake and deliver her special creations to people who truly appreciated it.

"Carissa! Hey everyone, Carissa's here!" Davey shuffled out with knobby knuckles raised to the height of his chest and arms wide open. "Let me help you with that."

"I think I better carry them inside. Last time, half the box was gone by the time you reached the table." She leaned into half hug Davey and lifted an elbow to greet the others since her hands were full.

"You'd deny a dying old geezer like me his sugar fix?" Davey puckered out his bottom lip.

"Please, you move better than a five-year-old at a dance recital."

"You got that right, little missy." Davey tapped his way to the table. His joints were frozen in position, but his feet sure did move with lightning speed. He removed his gray, pinstriped driving hat and took a bow.

The elder women flocked around Davey, hooking hands into the crooks of his elbows. He didn't mind. He plopped his hat back on his thinning silver hair and escorted the ladies to their seats.

"What do we have today? Oh, my word, they smell delicious. Did you get the job, Cassie dear?"

She loved how they all called her that, as if it were her name. "Not yet." The entire town knew their financial future rested on her shoulders. If only she could pass the torch. She'd try to convince Mr. Lancaster the minute she spoke to him alone, but for now, she was their only shot and she wouldn't let them down.

"Job? You mean that Hollywood donkey manure they are slinging at us? I, for one, say no to the uppity movie people. They're gonna ruin this town if they can. Trust me." Davey folded his arms over his chest and grunted.

Ms. Gina fluffed her orange hair and offered a tight-lipped coral smile. "Well, we were chatting, and we think that if we all decide to give the green light, we know you would be perfect for the big first episode they planned."

"We better do the production, 'cause Grandma needs a new Bingo basket." Mrs. Malter thumped her way over with her walker.

Ms. Gina, a former Las Vegas show girl, waved a theatrical hand in the air. "They should film a segment with us. After all, we're the true heart of the community."

"You mean true headache," Mrs. Malter grumbled.

Carissa opened the boxes, and the other ten seniors moved like they were twenty-two instead of eighty-two plus. She loved seeing their eyes light up. If only people would sit and have a cookie for five minutes instead of being buried in their phones or computers, the world would be a better place.

Perhaps she should tap on the door upstairs and offer some to Drew and Lori. She abandoned the idea, deciding one rejection of her desserts was enough for now.

"Ah, I should've known it was you." Thelma, their nurse, waved her hands about, shooing all the elders away from the sweets. "Only take one. Last time it was like I brought back toddlers from an amusement park. Talk about sugar high."

"Stop treating us like children," Mrs. Malter snapped.

"You're not children. You broke your hip doing a high-kicking routine when we returned to the center after your last sugar binge."

"Don't know what you're talking about." Mrs. Malter snagged a cookie, a cupcake, and a brownie, shoved them into her pocket, and scooted her walker faster than a getaway rocket.

"Sorry, Thelma. I hope you don't mind. I made all this for the production team as part of a pseudo-audition, but apparently the main guy doesn't eat sugar." The bitterness in Carissa's voice obviously caught Davey's attention.

He dropped his cookie and put up his fists. "Who's this despicable man? I'll put him in his place."

"Don't worry. I've got it covered. For the next tasting I'll use cayenne pepper instead of cinnamon."

"Oh, you got Jackie so good that time." Davey doubled over with a dramatic laugh. One that ended with a dry cough.

"Calm yourself, Mr. Samson." Thelma snagged a cookie. "Better get some before the others devour them."

"I'm calm. Don't fret. It makes lines on that pretty face of yours, Thelma." Davey was such a flirt. "Don't trust a man who doesn't eat sugar. Next thing you're gonna tell me is he only eats salads with dressing on the side. Sissy."

"Now, Davey. That's not nice," Carissa scolded but in a light-hearted, I-totally-agree tone.

He knew it, too, because he did a tap routine over to Ms. Gina, where he handed her a cupcake and snuggled into her side.

Carissa rolled her eyes. "You know, I think he was born a player."

"I think you're right." Thelma took a bite and offered an eyebrow raise. "Yum. Are these a new recipe? I love the sugar maple kind of flavor."

"Thanks. I've been experimenting. With flavor, at least."

"You've got a winner here." Thelma took another bite.

"Now if I could just make them look as pretty as they taste."

"Why you gotta do that for?" Davey asked.

"You can't hear me tell you to go to bed at night when I'm standing a foot from you, but you heard that from across the room?" Thelma huffed.

"I got my hearing aid turned on. I always turn it off when I know you're gonna tell me to do something I don't want to do." Davey reached up and turned his hearing aid off.

"Davey had a good question, though," Thelma said.

"Well, it needs to look pretty, according to Mr. Lancaster, the man who's in charge. He says viewers can't taste or smell the product, so I have to make them look like they taste and smell good."

"What's he want you to do? Put pretty flowers on top? Told ya, he's a sissy." Davey reached for his ear again, but who knew if he actually turned it off or not. He spun away from them to face the wall, giving Thelma and Carissa his back for added emphasis that he wasn't listening any longer.

Thelma didn't bite anyway. "Ignore him. If you give him attention, it only reinforces his behavior."

They both waited for a reply, but nothing, so Carissa sighed and sat at the table. "I know how to bake and make things taste good, but let's face it, in the superficial department, I get a big fat F. I'm not one to even fuss over *myself*. Heck, half the time I can't even find my hairbrush, let alone curl my hair or put on makeup. Who has time for that stuff anyway?"

Thelma drummed her fingers on the table. "Hmm...I wish I had an answer for you, hon."

"I have an answer, but no one ever asks me anything." Mrs. Malter picked up her walker and slammed it down against the old wood floor like a judge's mallet.

Carissa knew Mrs. Malter was once important and now she struggled with being in a home, especially when her family never came to visit her except on her birthday. "What's that? I could really use your help."

Mrs. Malter's peach lips curled into a devious grin. "We tar and southernize him."

"Those are fighting words." Thelma shook her head. "You don't mean that."

"Southernize him! Southernize him!" Davey chanted, and Ms. Gina joined in, a little off on the rhythm, though.

"Okay, okay, calm down. I'm surprised at you, Davey. I thought you were a gentleman." Carissa winked at him.

He put his fists up. "I can't let some stranger get you upset. I'm your knight with shining hair." Davey removed his cap and bowed.

"Remember, we need Mr. Lancaster to want to be here. I don't think what you guys are planning is going to help the situation."

"Told ya, we don't need those stuffy city folks. We've been just fine here in Sugar Maple for well over a hundred years. Done just fine, and we'll keep doing just fine." Mrs. Malter stood and waved her hand, spitting with her enthusiasm.

"Calm down. Remember your heart condition," Thelma said.

"What's going on in here?" Mr. Lancaster entered the room with his perfect hair, pressed shirt, and tight jaw.

"Take off your shoes. You got mud. I ain't gonna pay for a cleaning crew to come clean up after ya," Davey yelled.

Drew studied his shoes, but despite the fact there wasn't a speck of mud on them, he still removed them, something Carissa wasn't expecting, considering his earlier attitude.

She had to admit though, Drew looked more relaxed and approachable standing in his wool socks. "You need to be careful down here. The floor is old and worn. You could get a splinter."

"Good. Then he'll be easier to tar and southernize!" Davey hollered.

Mr. Lancaster strutted farther into the room. "What does that mean?" Two steps into the doorway, he hollered, grabbed his foot, and bounced around until he fell into the wall. "Ow!"

"She warned you, but those big city folks never listen." Ms. Gina waved her partners in crime over to a table to play some more bingo.

Carissa raced over to Mr. Lancaster. "I'm sorry about that. Here, sit down." She helped him over to the chair. The large man was leaning on her and hopping on one foot.

He collapsed and held his foot up to his knee. "This place is a hazard. Why hasn't it been torn down? The radiator upstairs doesn't work well, and now I've been impaled by a spear."

"Shh. Don't say such things. They might hear you." Carissa knelt in front of him and analyzed the damage. It was a large piece of wood, but it didn't appear to be too deep. It was hard to tell through the sock, though.

"Why? What is this tar and southernize thing they were chanting? Should I be worried?" Drew smiled and looked over at the elders.

She took advantage of his distraction and yanked the piece of wood out. "Yes, you should."

He rubbed his toe and grimaced like a schoolboy. So much for looking like he was perfect.

"Wait here, Mr. Lancaster. I'll be right back. You should clean your foot and make sure there aren't any small splinters left."

Thelma waved Carissa toward her bag. "Take what you need from my supplies, even though I don't think you should be providing aid to the enemy."

Drew removed his sock, sending gray wool lint onto the floor. "I'm not the enemy. I'm here to help."

"You've got a funny way of showing that you want this to work out." Carissa sat in the chair by his side and analyzed his toe. "Doesn't look like there's anything else in there. Oh, wait. I do see something." She retrieved a needle and tweezers from the bag. "This might hurt a little, but you need to get this out."

"I guess we did get off on the wrong foot, and I apologize for that." He held out his hand. "Miss Carissa Donahue, I'm Drew Lancaster, and it's a pleasure to meet you."

Carissa eyed his hand suspiciously but decided there was no way around pleasantries if they were going to be working together. "Nice to meet you, Mr. Lancaster."

"Drew. You can call me Drew." He wiggled under the needle when she dug a little deeper. "I can get this out later. Right now, I need to go meet the town elders. I think I need to make a better impression on the old people than I did on you."

"The what?" Davey spun like a Tasmanian devil with eyes as dark as a bat's. "Old? I ain't too old to tar and southernize you!"

CHAPTER FIVE

CARISSA KNELT in front of Drew, tending to his wound. She had a gentle touch, and despite the needle pricking his toe, he found her more agreeable than earlier. Perhaps it was because she didn't have her flock of friends around. "Thank you for your help, but you haven't answered my question. What was the geriatric gang chanting about?"

"Shh. Don't let them hear you call them that." The needle went in deeper, and he swore she did it on purpose. He winced, but she sat back and analyzed his toe, giving him room to breathe.

"It was a threat based on an old town legend." Carissa's hair floated like an unruly lioness mane around her face, but at least she wore a pullover sweater so there were no mismatched buttons.

"What kind of legend?" he asked, finding himself enjoying the distraction from the crazy mayor he had to deal with, the ridiculous project he'd been assigned, and his assistant's overbearing ways.

"It says that about eighty years ago, a man was accused of chopping down his wife's perfect maple tree that her grandfather had planted. She was so mad that she demanded he be arrested for spousal abuse."

"For cutting down a tree?" Drew rubbed his forehead, trying to process the madness.

She lit up like the first lights of Christmas on Rodeo Drive. "Oh, yes. We take maple extremely seriously in our town. After about a month of the sheriff dealing with various domestic calls, putting him in a cell for the night, where the man's snoring drove him insane, he decided to end the feud and went to speak to the wife."

He was thankful when Carissa finally got the splinter out, wiped his toe with the alcohol wipe, and bandaged the wound. She was like a pretty but disheveled Florence Nightingale. "So, what did the sheriff do to the woman?"

"The woman? Oh no, that's not who was tarred and southernized." She handed him his sock and sat in the chair by his side.

He wanted to reach up and brush the hair from her eyes that she didn't seem to notice but decided not to, proving Lori wrong about his OCD. "Really? I'm confused."

"You're not southern." She crumpled up the trash and tossed it into a bag at his side instead of the trash can where it belonged, but he didn't say anything.

"No, I'm not." Drew slid his foot into his sock but kept his ankle resting on his other knee.

"Well, the sheriff wouldn't keep him anymore, and it was getting too cold to sleep outside. He'd slept on all the couches of all the people in town who would have him, but his snoring was apparently so bad no one else would take him in."

"So much for southern hospitality," he teased.

She laughed, a cute, simple laugh that didn't hurt his ears. It was musical.

"There are limits to hospitality, even in Sugar Maple. Anyway, he decided he wanted to go home, but she said she didn't believe he was sorry. The town wouldn't take him, his wife wouldn't take him, so he decided to make her believe his apology and did it southern style."

"He tarred and feathered himself?"

"No. Not exactly." She waved her hands in front of her face, causing her shirt to shift out of place under her sweater, but she didn't notice. "He covered himself in maple syrup and leaves then stood outside of their home where the tree had been."

"That's how he apologized?"

"Sort of. That's where the southernized portion comes in. He handwrote a note on each leaf. *I shall not cut down any trees. I will do the dishes for six weeks. I will drink sweet tea and like it. I will never hurt my wife again. I will always be a southern gentleman.* There were dozens upon dozens of leaves on him."

"That's insane. Why would any man degrade himself in such a way?" He'd heard men do absurd things to win a girl before, but that was on an entirely new level.

"Because he loved her." She looked up at him. Her beautiful blue eyes were something he could photograph and sell to the world.

The geriatric gang snickered and pointed over their way. "Told ya he's a sissy. Needed to be doctored for a little splinter." Davey said loud and clear.

Carissa sat up on her knees and scooped up a box from the floor. "Legend has it that they renewed their vows two weeks later and they never fought again."

"Sounds like a small-town myth to me." The way she shoved her hair behind her shoulders and tossed the box in the large trash can told him she didn't agree with his observation.

"Well, believe what you want. I need to get back to work."

He hopped up and offered his hand to her, but she stood on her own. "Thanks for the doctoring."

"Sure. No problem." She grabbed her coat and hat. "Help yourself if you want something. Thelma would appreciate you taking away some temptation before the residents of the Sugar and Spice Home return on a sugar high." She left her chair out and headed for the door. "Never mind. I forgot you don't eat sugar."

"Don't eat sugar?" Davey shouted. "Don't trust a man who don't eat sugar. Told you he was a sissy."

"Be nice, Davey. Remember, we insult people with kindness around here." Carissa stopped in the doorway. "If you're hungry, they have a great chef salad at Maple Table."

"Really?"

Davey slapped his knees and rolled with laughter. "Told you!"

Carissa grinned with an inside-joke smile and disappeared into the entryway.

Fine, if these people wanted to make a joke out of him, he didn't care.

He headed for the stairs, but at the bottom step he realized that he had a job to do. A job that would get him out of Knox Brevard's team and onto a real project. Fine, he'd swallow his pride. He about faced and marched to where Carissa was snugging her hat down onto her head, which made the ends of her hair staticky and rise like horns in her back.

"Listen, why don't I take you to dinner tonight to discuss what changes can be made to your desserts to make them more visibly appealing? I can pick you up in an hour."

"No thanks." Carissa opened the door and took the steps two at a time.

"Wait. What do you mean, no?" He raced outside after her. The cold bit at his nose and toes.

"I'm busy."

Apparently he needed to turn up the charm to make up for his less than southern ways. "Too busy to eat? I mean, I'd like to take you to a nice restaurant."

She approached him with a gleam in her eye. There, he had her now.

"Are you asking me out on a date, Drew Lancaster?"

He glanced at the window above the center, where he caught Lori staring down at them before she shut the curtains. Fine, he'd prove he wasn't all work and no play. "Yes, I'd like to take you out tonight."

Carissa leaned into him and tilted her head to one side as if reading his thoughts. "You have the wrong girl. Now I know for sure you should work with my dear old friend Jacqueline. But for now, I'll meet with your assistant tomorrow morning at eight. Until then, Mr. Lancaster, have a pleasant evening."

He stood there in the cold, watching Carissa walk across the town square until his feet were number than his thoughts. Dang... Did he just get rejected by a girl he would never want to date in the first place? He hightailed it inside, where he found the geriatric gang laughing at him. But he didn't stop, not until he was in the office facing Lori. "This is your fault."

She slid her glasses down her nose and peered over them. "Ah, I see."

"No, you don't. But you will when you have to meet with that woman tomorrow morning. That's when you'll realize this project is the dumbest idea Knox has ever concocted."

"No." Lori set her laptop down on the table and sat forward.

"What do you mean, no?" Drew went to the radiator and held his hands out to the metal contraption.

"We have a deal. You need to attend the meeting, and you need to take Carissa Donahue on a few dates."

"No way." He touched the radiator, but it was cold again. "Enough of this place. We need to cut our losses and tell Knox this is not happening."

"You won't or you can't because she turned you down?"

He huffed, eyeing the bake shop through the window. "She only did that to make a point."

"What point is that?"

He shrugged. "I don't know. She's southern. I don't get these people. Besides, you chose wrong. I'll give you a shot to change your mind. I mean, there's no way in this godforsaken town that I would ever fall for a woman like that. She's too...too—"

"Perfect."

"Perfect? Ha! Do you know she left trash out, and that hair! It is everywhere. It's as if she doesn't even notice things are a mess around her."

"As I said, she's perfect for you. I stand by my choice. You get her to go out with you and you don't fall in love with her, then I'll call my father. That's it."

"This is insane and wrong. I won't make a bet about a woman."

She stood, brushing the wrinkles out of her pants like a normal person would. "Why, Drew Lancaster, I think you've finally met your romantic match. I think you're scared you can't win her over with your quick wit and charm. For once, Drew can't rely on his sexy smile and good looks. This woman doesn't fall for the visual attractiveness but on truth of something."

"What are you babbling about?"

"Think about it. She's a baker. She cares about the smell and taste. You're a movie and TV guy who only cares about the appearance of things. You don't stand a chance. You're all looks and no substance."

Lori snagged her purse and headed for the stairs.

"Where are you going?"

She slung the strap over her arm but didn't stop her movement. "I'm going to my room at the inn. The nice room these townspeople gave us in order to make us feel at home. You can continue to hide up here for now, or you can come enjoy some down time by the warm fire and work in the parlor."

"I don't have time for that." Drew huffed. "I need to go meet with the geriatric gang downstairs."

Lori paused and glanced over her shoulder. "I wouldn't lead with that."

"I'm not an idiot, you know." He ran his hands through his

hair and let out a long, deep, calming breath.

"You sure about that? From what I hear, you need to get those people downstairs on our side, or when Knox arrives, you won't have a show to present at all." Lori clomped down the stairs, and he followed close behind, determined to show those people downstairs the upside to their proposal.

At the bottom of the steps, he caught sight of Davey two stepping with one of the ladies. Drew straightened his collar and checked his hair in the mirror hanging on the wall. It couldn't be that difficult to convince some old people to sign off on a project that would benefit the town they loved. This was the easiest sale ever.

Yet his stomach knotted with warning like it did when they would enter a new city, not knowing who was friendly and who was the enemy.

The song finished blaring over the crackling speakers, so Drew took his opportunity and marched to the center of the room. "Sir, since you are obviously the man in this town who makes all the important decisions, I'd like to request a meeting with you. Perhaps I could take you to dinner this evening to discuss the benefits of this project and how it will stir new life into this great little town."

Davey adjusted his cap as if he was at the start of a race. "I don't have time for a dinner meeting. Have your people call my people to set up an appointment. I have an opening sometime next month, I think."

Davey snugged his cap down and headed for the door. "Let's go. I've had enough dancing for one evening." And as if he had control over the rest of the gang and employees, they all followed his lead.

He'd seen enough unassuming children and elderly masking deadly weapons to know Davey wasn't just an innocent old man. He was carrying a vest full of explosives, and Drew was his main target.

CHAPTER SIX

"I KNEW I'd find you already baking." Stella rolled in with a sprinkling of snow. "What time did you start?"

Carissa closed the display case and wiped her hands on her dish towel strung through her apron. "Four." She wasn't in the mood for an inquisition, but she knew Stella meant well.

"That's all you've baked since four?" Stella hovered over the case, looking down at the selection. "Ah...what's that?"

"It's a cupcake with almond-flavor frosting." She eyed the so-called masterpiece she'd spent hours perfecting.

"I mean those things sprinkled on top." Stella pointed as if a rat who died mid nibble sat on top.

"Those are edible sugar pearls." Carissa slid the tie from her hair and removed her apron but kept a rag tight in her hands, glad to have a minute to rest and collect herself before her meeting with Lori.

"It looks so...weddingish." Stella's nose squished like she was allergic to the word. Not that Carissa was a fan either.

She studied her creation; had she missed the mark? "Yes, but it's pretty and will photograph well."

The heat cut on with a blast of warmth that could melt any

frosting. Stella glanced at the vent with the I've-got-to-fix-that lip press. But obviously deciding the task at hand took precedence, she walked around the cupcake, analyzing it from all corners. "Who says?"

"Several articles about top pastry chefs had this exact cupcake shown." Carissa collapsed into a chair. "Why? Is it not pretty enough?"

Stella sat across from her. She didn't take Carissa's hand the way Felicia would or pat her shoulder like Ms. Horton, but she sat by her side, which was a big deal for Stella. The girl couldn't bond with a puppy without cringing away from it a hundred and two times first. "Listen, it's beautiful, but it isn't you. Can't you make something that's pretty that is more you? We want you to win, but not if you have to sell your soul to Hollywood."

The heat cut out. Stella crunched her face with determination to return later to defeat that darn radiator issue. Like most things in Sugar Maple, the radiator was ancient but comforting.

The wind outside whistled through the crack above the front door, sending a chill into the room. "This isn't about me. It's about winning this show for the town. I think this is what they want for their show." Carissa rubbed her temples, trying to relieve the tension.

Stella patted the table next to her hand. "You're not alone. We all have your back. As much as the town needs this, we all need you more. Don't be something you're not to win this. Let the world see Carissa Donahue as the angel she is to all of us. You are the sweetest, most giving person I know. Show that."

"Are you Felicia dressed as Stella?" Carissa asked, easing her death grip on the poor defenseless hand towel.

Stella did her breath-out-of-the-side-of-her-mouth thing she did when she was uncomfortable sharing sentiment with someone. "Please, you know you're an angel. You stayed here after high school to help me. Don't think I didn't know. I'm just glad you managed to fix this old place up and make it your own, or I would've felt guilty for the rest of my life."

"I didn't have anywhere to go. This is my home." Carissa never wanted Stella to feel responsible for her choices. They were her own. Yes, maybe she made them out of love for a friend, but she was more than just a friend. She was better than family because she stayed after everyone else had left her. "You didn't abandon me either, remember? When you were offered the apprenticeship at that fancy car repair place in Nashville, you turned it down to stay here. I knew you wanted to get out of this town."

"I couldn't leave. We were rebuilding this place." Stella pointed at the exposed wood beams overhead and the antique display case she'd helped repair. "And it's perfect. It's you."

"We'll call it even, then." Carissa patted her fingers before Stella pulled away and stood, shoving both hands safely in her pocket.

The old clock that was a gift from Felicia on opening day of her bakery chimed with warning. "I need to finish up. Lori will be here any minute."

"I'll get out of your way, then." Stella paused. "Um, did you get a chance to make the maple bacon donuts this morning?"

"I'm afraid not. I promise, I'll bring you some this afternoon." Carissa wiped down the tables and straightened the chairs, deciding it was time to face the Knox brigade coming to criticize her baked goods.

"No, don't worry about it. I'll be out at the Hendrix farm repairing a tractor this afternoon."

"Hey, at least you have business." Carissa pointed to the empty bistro chairs.

Stella nodded. "I know it's the worst month of the year for you. Not only because of the business." She opened the door, leaving her words hanging in the air like a noose around failed relationships. "Just remember, you're perfect."

The door shut before Carissa could protest. Perfection was one thing she'd never be in her life. This cupcake had to be what they were looking for, though. It was all the rage, right? Then why did she feel empty inside each time she looked at it?

Carissa set out her special china serving dishes and plated the cupcake with a confection flower she'd made this morning. The yellow added color to the plate so it didn't look so...boring.

She didn't want to admit it to herself, but that wasn't a treat she'd choose. The appearance didn't draw her to want to try it. But this wasn't about her, it was about the town. That Drew Lancaster had gotten into her head with all the appearance mumbo jumbo he was spouting.

The front doorbell chimed, announcing a visitor. "Good morning." A bright and cheerful Drew entered. He looked different, dressed in casual yet perfectly pressed pants. "It smells delicious in here. Is that almonds?"

"You smell that?" Her interest piqued. The man knew the aroma of something beyond expensive perfume and fine Italian leather.

"Yes, of course. Almonds always get my attention. Here." He kicked the door shut behind him with a loud thud and held out a coffee from Mary-Beth's shop, Maple Grounds. "She said this is your favorite."

Carissa stood there, trying to reconcile the man in front of her with the one she'd met the other day. Sure, he was dressed more casually, and his hair wasn't gelled back like a 1950s greaser, but it was still perfect. "Who are you, and what did you do with the party planner? Sorry, executive producer person."

He laughed, but it sounded forced, like someone was controlling him.

"Wait, I watched a movie like this once. The outsider went mad when trapped in a hotel..." She tossed the rag behind the register.

"That was *The Shining*, and we're not in the northwest. I think you're safe." He set the cup down on the table in front of her when she didn't immediately take it and dropped his bag in the chair. "It looks like you've been working hard."

He pointed to her shirt. Great. Somehow the flour had managed to slip past her apron barrier. She brushed it off and realized her hands were shaking, so she grabbed the cup and took a long sip from it before she answered. "Yes, well, I think you'll like the appearance of what I made. Here, sit down." She remembered he didn't eat sugar, but she placed a fork down next to his plate anyway and stood over him, waiting for his response.

Except for the ticking clock on the wall and the hum of the refrigerator in the kitchen, the room was silent. "So, um…what is this?"

Carissa swallowed, trying to come up with fancy jargon that made her sound like a professional pastry chef. "It's a buttery, moist vanilla cake covered in a whipped buttercream frosting with a touch of almond." Did she say butter twice?

"Ah, that's where the almond is coming from." He glanced up at her with an apprehensive look. "Why don't you sit down, and we'll talk about this one."

She saw it, the way his jaw twitched. This wasn't good news. "What don't you like? It's what's on all the New York bakery websites and magazine advertisements. I did a market study last night to figure out what you were looking for." She collapsed into the chair at his side and held tight to Mary-Beth's homemade hot chocolate with maple syrup and pumpkin spice.

"You know about market research?"

She shrugged. "Just because I didn't go to college doesn't mean I haven't learned anything. I've been studying over the years on how to run a bakery, both in marketing and in baking. Unfortunately, in a small town, marketing is a little different."

"I see." He turned the plate, analyzing all the way around as if to find the best angle for filming. "Well, it's perfect for a wedding shoot, or a New York bakery advertisement."

A hint of hope gave her the feeling of a sugar rush after a morning tasting session in the kitchen.

"That being said, it isn't perfect for what we're looking for specifically for this campaign."

She let out a long breath. "I guess Stella was right. She seems to know what you want, so maybe you should be working with her."

"Thank goodness that wasn't Lori's pick," he mumbled.

"What?"

He shifted in his chair. "Nothing. I'm just saying you're the right person for the job. We just need to work to figure this out."

"I'm confused. I thought this is what you wanted. Something that looked neat and pretty."

"Yes, I can see that you did your homework." He lifted his fork and slid it into the top of the frosting.

"I thought you didn't eat sugar," she said in a self-saboteur way.

"I don't. I tend to control what I put in my body to stay healthy."

Davey would've loved that opening for a good joke.

"But I ran an extra couple of miles this morning."

"Of course you did." Carissa rolled her eyes.

A beep sounded in the back, reminding her of the scones for the bingo session today. "Excuse me, I'll be right back." She raced to the kitchen, grabbed the oven mitt, and set the scones out on a cooling rack before returning to the front.

Drew sat hunched over the plate, devouring the cupcake like a two-year-old. It was the best compliment he could've given her. A warmth spread in her chest while she watched him enjoy her food.

It had been a long time since she had anyone around to savor her baking. Sure, Davey and the ladies at the home loved them, but they were on special diets and only enjoyed treats when she brought them to their events. But the last time she'd seen anyone enjoy something she made the way Drew was now was when her grandfather was alive. God rest his soul.

Drew's gaze darted to her. He tossed his fork down and wiped his mouth with the cloth napkin. "You know, this isn't just a New York bakery cupcake or even a wedding treat. It's unique. And that almond. It isn't just an almond extract."

"It is. It's just that I make it myself." Carissa sat and enjoyed a few sips of hot chocolate as he studied his hands and fingers before placing the napkin on the table.

"It's unique but feels like home. I haven't tasted anything like that since my Aunt Sally passed away. She had a family recipe that was brought over here from Germany, and every holiday she'd make it. There was a spice and an almond flavor to it that I've never tasted since. This has that almost roasted almond flavor."

He lit up talking about his family and the food they once shared. It turned out Drew Lancaster was a real human.

"That's what I try to do with my baking, bring family memories back into focus, make people feel loved."

Drew leaned back in the small chair. His large frame made the room feel cozy. "I never thought of food that way. Especially not desserts. Maybe a turkey or something that everyone has at the holidays, but not a dessert."

"I'm not talking about normal stuff. It's the kind of food that reminds us of our childhoods, full of hugs and safety and unconditional love."

He leaned toward Carissa. "There is something different about you. I can't figure it out, though." A laugh escaped his lips, filling the room with happiness.

"What is it?" she asked.

"Nothing. I just thought maybe if I could bake like this, I could actually get Davey and the rest of the geriatric gang to speak with me about this project. If not, according to your mayor, I won't have a show to produce."

Carissa didn't know what Ms. Horton was up to with all that. Sure, the elders had a say, but they weren't the final vote.

He leaned closer as if to whisper a secret, but instead he pressed his finger to a crumb and lifted it to his lips. His closeness made her unable to think. How long had it been since she'd been this close to a man besides Davey? She couldn't sit still; her nerves were kicking into high gear. Baking...she needed to bake. "Come. I can show you what I meant and help you with Davey."

She snagged her apron and headed for the kitchen. Before she began, she washed her hands, tied her apron neatly around her waist, and pulled her hair back into a low bun.

Drew stood there watching her with mouth ajar. His gaze was intense and searching, as if trying to reconcile something.

"What?"

"It's nothing."

She gave him the yeah-right look.

His gaze broke away and scanned the cookie jar that Ms. Horton had given her for her nineteenth birthday, the fish bowl Stella won for her at the county fair that was now filled with dried flowers from Mary-Beth, next to it the stuffed animal Jacqueline made for her when she had her tonsils out in second grade. "It's just that you look so put together right now. Your hair. You should wear it like that more often. It allows your pretty face to be seen."

A flush rushed up her neck and to her cheeks. Oven... She needed to turn back on the oven. "There's another apron on the hook right there."

"I think it's best you do this part on your own. You bake, I take the pictures." He retrieved his bag and produced a camera.

Carissa's internal heater stoked to five hundred degrees. Now wasn't the time to shove a lens in her face. "You don't have anything to take a picture of right now, so you can help." Carissa took out two baking sheets and a large mixing bowl. This had to work. No need to let the guy know she wasn't photogenic. Not since she won the department store magazine cover in third grade. The one that put a rift between Jackie and her for four months. A lifetime to be in friendship jail when a kid is nine years old.

She forced a calming breath and reminded herself that he only wanted pictures of food, not her. "You're about to experience what I mean."

"I'm not following."

"You, my friend, are about to win over the toughest critic in town." She shoved a wooden spoon at him. "I'll put the ingredients in there, and you can mix. When we're done, you can go with me to give these to Davey."

"You mean go back to that crazy group of geriatric patients?" He put the spoon in the bowl and stepped back as if it had turned into an angry blow torch. "I'm not sure I'm ready for that yet. I need a plan of action before I enter that minefield."

"What's wrong? They aren't perfect enough for you?" Carissa knew it was time this guy understood what this town was all about. Only then would she know for sure he wasn't going to put these people through an obstacle course, only to end the race before they could reach the finish line.

"No, I mean...they're fine. It's just that..." Drew didn't stand in his perfect stance. Instead, he fidgeted with the camera.

"What?" Carissa tapped her foot. No one messed with the elders of their town.

Drew ran an uncharacteristic hand through his hair, causing it to separate before it popped back into place. "They scare me."

Carissa laughed, a real laugh she felt deep down to her toes. It relaxed her, and for the moment Drew didn't seem so corporate and serious. "You do realize that Davey is a quarter of your size and about three times your age."

"Maybe, but he's...well, southern." He winked.

A wink that shot a heat wave through her. She shifted between her feet. "Then you better get started, because in the south, we use food to connect with people. You never attend a wake without food, or a party, or a Christening, or a church picnic without food. It's the law of the south. And Drew Lancaster, you need to lose some corporate attitude and learn some southern hospitality if you're going to make this work. In other words, be less...you."

CHAPTER SEVEN

WHEN CARISSA FINALLY STOPPED LAUGHING, she tied a plain white apron around his waist and shoved the mixing bowl and spoon into his chest. "They say it's best to face your fears, so let's get started. It's time that you take an offering to the elders."

She was not going to take no for an answer, and he promised Lori he'd be accepting of others. Drew rolled his sleeves up to three-quarters, below his elbows but high enough not to smudge them. "Why do I have an image of me strapped to a stake over a pile of wood?"

"They wouldn't do that." She half shrugged. "But I can't guarantee they won't pull another trick on you."

He placed his camera in the bag, realizing there really wasn't anything to photograph at the moment. Nothing even for test shots. Except for the beautiful woman in the apron, but something told him she wouldn't be comfortable with him taking photographs of her. "You do know that we're supposed to be working. I have a call this afternoon with Knox Brevard, and I need to tell him where we're at on this project." The heaviness of his words caused a tightness in the muscles in the back of his neck.

"I don't know what to tell you. I'm just the baker." Carissa danced around the kitchen like a nutcracker fairy at the ballet. This was her element, her happy place. If only he could find his happy place. He'd been unsettled for most of his life. Ever since returning from Iraq, he worked and had a nice apartment but never felt at home. He hadn't been home since he lived in California with his aunt the summer before he left to join the Corp.

A yellow-hued light above flooded over Carissa like a spotlight. He couldn't help himself, so he retrieved his camera and snapped a shot of her.

She froze, as if her world had been shattered by the clicking of his camera.

"Put that away, or I'll toss it in the oven. Got me?" She didn't back down, which he could respect. Not that he wouldn't try again later, but for now, he returned the camera to the bag and set it in the corner. He'd underestimated Carissa. She was a handful and a half, as his aunt Sally used to say. Focus. That's what he needed to do. "As nice as that sounds, we need to make this project work."

"You say that as if you need it to work as much as we do." Carissa raised her brows at him.

He set the bowl down and lifted the spoon out of the way. "Perhaps we can whip this up quick and then I can take you to lunch to discuss some ideas and review some images I pulled together for you." One social situation would show Lori he was on board and perhaps get her thinking about calling her father. It would get him back to California. Maybe he'd try to buy his aunt's old place and fix it up.

"Whip up quick?" She put a hand on her hip and gave him a one-two air slap with her eggbeater. "First of all, I never throw things together and rush them out the door. Secondly, I think best when I'm baking. And third, what is this obsession you have with taking me on a date?"

His throat gripped his words tight, but he forced them free. "Not a date. A working lunch."

She shot him a sideways glance. "Sure, working lunch."

This wasn't as easy as he'd thought it would be. Since when did a girl not want to eat lunch with him? "Fine. We'll bake... What are we baking?"

"Southern Man Bars." There it was again, that grin that told him there was more to this than she was sharing. But he wasn't getting anywhere forcing her to work, so maybe he needed to follow Lori's advice and try to make friends instead of treating them like clients. He had a few hours, and he'd had tighter deadlines in the past.

"And what are those?"

"You'll see." She dumped some chocolate chips and graham crackers into the bowl without even measuring them.

"I guess you memorized the recipe." He wanted to count the number of dark morsels, but the graham crackers covered them.

She grabbed some nuts and some milk or cream from a carafe and some bottle that looked like vanilla extract. The woman was a tornado in the kitchen, something you couldn't help but look at, no matter how much chaos it caused in its path. "Nope, they are never exactly the same." With a hand to her chin, she looked around, and then she clapped her hands together once. "Ah, perfect." She snagged a container with what looked like a bunch of spices.

"What is that?"

She tossed things in like a witch brewing a potion in a horror film. Nothing organized, nothing measured, only a dash of ground eye of newt and a sprinkle of wool of bat.

"My top-secret fall spice collection."

"What's in it?" He attempted to gain some sort of measure on this project.

She dumped some into the bowl and then closed it. "That would be the secret part."

The light overhead flickered and sputtered. "If you have a ladder, I can fix that for you."

"Come on, start mixing." She smacked his hand with the eggbeater.

The bulb strobed but then settled into a bright light again. "Seriously, I don't mind. Doesn't that bother you?" He pointed at the fixture.

She followed his gaze to the ceiling, as if seeing the issue for the first time. "No, why would it? It's not out yet. Now stop avoiding your job. Mix already."

He stuck the spoon in and watched the junkyard of ingredients roll over each other. "Can't we just toss this into an electric mixer?"

She gasped as if a rat ran across the kitchen.

"What?"

"How dare you." She held her hand to her chest. "Nothing in this kitchen is made with less than my best effort. Each taste is only as good as the love I pour into it." Carissa disappeared for a moment into the closet, and he smashed and mushed all the ingredients together. The inefficient process of hand mixing caused bits of graham cracker to flick out of the bowl and smear down his front. He stopped and grabbed a dish towel and smudged it across the white apron.

"What happened?" She set two containers on the counter.

He continued to battle the spot, but it didn't fade at all. "There's some gunk on me."

She grabbed her dish towel and flicked him in the arm with it. "Seriously? Gunk?"

"I didn't mean—"

"Get over yourself and get back to mixing. It's not like you have flour all over your shirt or face. You wear an apron for a reason. You're not baking if the front of you isn't stained with something."

He wanted to tell her this wasn't organized and efficient, but he figured he better not open his mouth again or he might end up like Hansel or Gretel.

"Not like that." Her hand covered his wrist.

A quick zap shot from her touch up his arm, and his pulse double timed. No, not possible. This girl couldn't elicit any kind of physical response. It was a reaction to an unexpected touch, that's all. Like discovering a combatant.

She guided his arm with smooth strokes around the bowl, each turn heating his skin a little more. "You're not beating it to death. You're combining the ingredients."

His heart quickened, either at the closeness or from beating the concoction in his bowl into submission. This didn't compute. It had to be a side effect of the work stress or Lori cramming bad ideas into his head. "I'm sorry, but this doesn't look appetizing. This is the geriatric favorite?"

"Stop referring to them as geriatric patients. They are town elders, and the ones who are still on the town council are Davey, Mrs. Malter, and Ms. Gina."

He had to admit the way her forehead crinkled and her eyes narrowed was adorable in a strange, nonsymmetrical way.

He set the bowl down and put some space between himself and Carissa. All this heat and the smells and conversation mixed him up. He needed to keep the conversation light and informational. The more he understood about the town, the smoother this project would go.

"So why do you refer to Davey by his first name and the ladies by their last?"

"Davey isn't his real name. He just likes to be called that because he loves to dance like Sammy Davis Junior. I called him Davey once years ago when he asked me to dance with him at a party. It stuck. Everyone else is an elder, so it's a sign of respect to call them by their last names—or in Ms. Gina's case, her stage name." She pointed at the scary mess in front of him again.

He mixed a little more, but the batter was tough. There was

no way he'd be trying these. "I don't know what this is supposed to look like, but I think I'm done here."

She took the bowl from him and dumped the batter over a parchment-lined pan, where she smashed it until it was level. It looked like something you'd find in a barn. "Your nose is crinkling. Stop looking at it and smell it."

The pan was in his face before he could step away, and he couldn't help but catch a whiff of fall by a fireside. "Okay, it does have a pleasant smell, but you can't capture a smell on camera."

She ignored his remark, slid the pan into the oven, and then handed him the bowl and spoon. "Time to clean up. And before you ask, no, I don't have a dishwasher."

"Why doesn't that surprise me?" He washed the mixing stuff and then removed the apron and set it on the counter, brushing off any stray graham cracker crumbs from his sleeves.

"You're not done." Carissa handed him a dish of white stuff with specs of spice in it and tossed the apron at his chest.

"What's this?"

"You need to make them look pretty when they come out of the oven. That's your specialty, right?" Carissa made some sort of glaze and drizzled it over what he assumed were scones and then put them in boxes. All that time, he watched how she moved with such grace. The woman was different in the kitchen, put together, angelic, beautiful, even if she still functioned like a Tasmanian Devil from that Bugs Bunny commercial he watched as a kid.

He tied the apron back around his middle, attempting to ignore the blemish of chocolate on the front. How in this little town was he going to make this work? Yes, Lori was right, he did need this win, but at what cost? His sanity?

"What are you mumbling about over there? You need to focus when baking."

"I don't mumble. And I'm focused on the task at hand."

"Then why are you ignoring the timer going off? If that burns, you're starting over." Carissa tossed an oven mitt at him. "Take them out and put them on top of the stove. Cut them, then roll them in the powdered sugar and spices, and then put them on that plate. You think you can handle that?"

He jumped into motion and managed to save the Southern Man Bars from ruin. Was he really cooking? No, he was working to get this done so he could get her to go to lunch with him for two reasons. One, to show her some images of the right kind of baked items that would work for the program, and two, his backup plan. Lori needed to see that he took her out on a date-non-date. How many did she say he had to go on anyway? He needed to clarify that when he returned to the inn this evening.

He and Carissa worked side by side in the cozy kitchen in the back of her bakery. The aroma of cinnamon and something that could only be described as home filled their world. Flashes of childhood baking with his aunt Sally motivated him to finish the bars, dipping them in sugar and then placing them on the plate. When finished, he had a feeling of accomplishment, something he hadn't felt in years. Perhaps not since going home during college.

"They look great. You did well."

Her praise unexpectedly soothed him. He didn't need validation for a job well done. He was paid bonuses for that. "What now?"

"We need to deliver them."

He hesitated. "I think it would be best if you gave these to them."

"What's wrong? You scared of a few elders?"

He dusted the powdered sugar from his hands. "No. It's just that I have to get back to work."

"You are working."

"No, I mean my real job." He untied his apron and set it on the countertop.

She blocked his exit. "You still don't get it. If you want this town to be on board with the filming, then you need to make sure you get the elders' stamp of approval."

"Fine, but once the contract is signed, they won't be able to cause any more disruptions. Speaking of the contract... We still need to get something for the test shots done by the end of the week. They're just preliminary. Someone else will be here once the contract is signed to do the promotional photo shoot and filming. That is if the test shots are approved and your bakery is chosen as the spotlight intro segment."

"We'll meet with Ms. Horton after we deliver these." Carissa covered the plate and snagged the boxes. "These need to be delivered while they're fresh. Let's go." She hooked her apron on the wall and went to the shop. "You can talk on our way."

"It's midmorning. Don't you need to get someone to man your shop?"

She glanced around the room and gave him an are-you-serious look. "I think if anyone has a sugar craving, they can wait a few minutes."

"You should care more about this project since your business is struggling so much. This program could bring needed revenue here to Sugar Maple."

"January is a slow month. My bakery was packed in the fall," she snipped, her southern accent dipping to a low drawl.

He blinked at her. "January is a great opportunity to sell new beginnings. Maybe that's something we can incorporate into your segment to add a little something extra."

"If we work together at all." Again, that irritated brow crunch and eye squinting told him he'd hit a nerve.

"I thought you were on board with this. The mayor said you were going to make the best product for the first segment." He retrieved his coat and snagged the one he assumed was Carissa's from the hook near the door and held it up for her.

"If there's a first segment. You're so sure that your only worry is how to get me to make something pretty for your filming, but if you don't get a contract, you won't have to worry about it." She shoved her arms into the coat and hiked it over her shoulders then stepped away from him.

"The mayor is on board. This is all but signed." Drew buttoned his coat and wrapped his scarf around his neck. "Come on. I get the dog and pony show. I have to please the elders to keep them happy, but they aren't really the decision makers for this town. No one is crazy enough to put the future of this town in the hands of a manipulating dancing man in a hat, a former show girl, and a cranky old lady."

"You still don't get it. We respect our elders here in town. They serve on a board that will vote on this project. We don't shove them in homes and forget about them here." She tugged the band from her hair, sending it into a wild frenzy until she shoved her hat over it and wrapped her scarf around her neck. "You seem to think that I wanted to spend my morning cooking with you because you are amazing and every woman would want to spend time with you. News flash... The mayor put me up to this, just like your assistant told you to come make nice."

He studied his coat, realizing he'd missed a button, so he quickly corrected it. "I don't know what you're talking about."

"What I'm saying is that if you don't take those treats in there and smooth things over with the elders you alienated yesterday, then you won't have to worry if I can make something pretty for your camera or if Jacqueline can make a beautiful dress, or Mary-Beth creates the perfect beverage, or Felicia arranges the perfect floral bouquet, or Stella fixes a carburetor, because this program will end."

CHAPTER EIGHT

THEY WERE UNLOADING the bus at the recreation room, so Carissa decided to go ahead and take the detour to her first stop. It would buy her some time to figure out how to convince Drew that she was the wrong place to start his production focus in Sugar Maple. There had to be a way to convince him. Although, if her feminine wiles didn't win him over, she wasn't sure she had a chance to make the man change his mind.

"You're going the wrong way." Drew hiked the strap of his camera bag up on his shoulder and held up the box of treats as if she'd forgotten about the mission to the recreation center.

"Nope. Going the right way." She didn't offer any other details since she didn't want to open it for debate.

"Okay, why are we headed toward the inn?" he asked.

She pointed to her box of scones. "To deliver these."

"Listen, I know you're trying to initiate me into this small-town clan, but why don't we at least stop at that café or I can take you to lunch." His voice shook from the cold or from hiding something.

Time to find out what his obsession with taking her to lunch was all about. If Ms. Horton was correct, directness would work best. "Why are you so determined to take me somewhere?"

"What?" His gaze shifted all over the I'm-lying zone. "Can't someone just need a bite to eat while they work?"

No, she wasn't buying his pitch. She studied him, watching him squirm and tug at his jacket collar with his free hand. The movement was so unDrew-like. She'd only known him a short time, but in five minutes she knew this man was a solid, nonfidgeting businessman.

A rumble of questions formed in her head. "Are you trying to throw me off my game so I'll convince the elders to approve this project without you having to work for it? News flash... Small-town folk respect hard work, not fancy promises."

"Ah, no. I, well. Yeah, that's it." He toed a crack in the sidewalk. "It's not uncommon to take clients out to eat to show them how interested we are."

"Interested?"

"In your business—the business, I mean." He eyed the elders being escorted off the bus. "Listen, it's fine. I'm great with grandparents. I'll win them over on my own. I realize now this isn't New York City and you're not the typical client."

"No, I'm not. Honesty and loyalty are the only things that'll get you going around here."

"I can do that. Be honest, I mean."

Honesty? She wasn't sure she bought that, but the game would continue between them until she could manage to steer him in the right direction. Maybe if she understood more about this filming and what they were looking for she'd be able to formulate a better plan. Not that plans were her strength. "Then tell me why this project is so important to you. Why are you willing to do work with a girl in a kitchen of a small-town bakery that obviously made you uneasy to get a contract to work with elders you don't like in a place you obviously don't want to be?"

"It's my job," he announced in a matter-of-fact, what-don't-you-get tone.

There was no use. The man wouldn't be honest if she hooked him up to a lie detector test and had his nana ask him questions. "Riiiight." She hotfooted it to the corner, down the street, over two blocks, and up the hill to the inn. "You would have an easier time if you just start at the fashion store with Jacqueline."

He stopped at the edge of the wrought iron fence surrounding the historic Victorian home. "She made that abundantly clear when we met at the coffee shop."

Carissa didn't have to ask what that meant. She knew her ex-best friend better than anyone. "Then why not?" She forced herself not to bite down so hard she'd chip a tooth again. It was strange to want to turn over something because you don't want it, yet giving it to the person you resented was a hard cupcake to swallow.

"Because she isn't right for the first segment. We need someone who is the essence of this town, who can show the camaraderie of the people."

"Then I'm definitely not the right person for the job." Her skin tingled, reminding her it was freezing outside and they needed to get indoors, so she headed up the brick sidewalk toward the inn.

"Tell me what's the deal with you two. I thought you were childhood friends, but there have been hints made about a falling out between you."

She rounded on him like a winter storm, bitter, cold, and relentless. "Leave that alone. Not part of the story. Got it?"

He took a step back. "Got it."

She forced a smile she was sure looked like that Stephen King clown on that horror movie. "Good. Let's go."

"Wait. Tell me why we're here. Are there going to be a mass of townspeople inside waiting with leaves and maple syrup?"

She laughed. A humor she hadn't felt in a long time tickled her with the image of children pasting leaves to his clothes.

"You'd have to be carried away in a strait jacket if gooey hands touched your perfect clothing."

She reached the steps.

"Wait."

"No more waiting. You're not going to weasel—"

"Shh." He held a black leather, stylish but too-thin gloved finger to his lips. "Do you hear that?"

She listened but didn't hear anything. "What?"

"That sound."

"What sound?"

He set his box on the front porch, stepped off the brick path, and walked around until he disappeared from her sight. "That."

Footprints marked his way, so she left her own box on the porch and followed him over the dormant rose bushes to the side of the inn. "Where are you going?"

He cupped his ear. "There." He pointed above his head. "It's coming from up there. I thought I heard it last night when Lori forced me to work at the inn's parlor. She said I was imagining it, but I'm not. Listen."

Mew. Mew.

"Is that a cat?" She scanned the roofline but didn't see it. The motherly draw to help filled her insides. "Poor thing must be stuck up there."

He removed his coat and scarf and tossed it to her. "I think you're right."

Mew. Mew. Mew. It cried and whined, stirring her into action.

"Poor thing." Carissa backed away, trying to see if it was close to the roof edge. "Should I call the fire department?"

"Let's see if we can get the poor thing down first." He climbed the oak tree that was the pride of the inn and managed to shimmy out onto a hearty branch toward the roof. A sight she'd never thought she'd see from Drew Lancaster. He wasn't the tree-climbing, rescuing cats kind of guy. This was the first time he'd surprised her since he'd arrived in town. "It's not on the roof."

A bitter wind gusted, shaking the tree. "I think it's in the chimney."

She pulled her cell from her back pocket. "I'll call the fire department." The icy air caused her fingers to shake, making it difficult to dial, but she managed to hit 911. "You better get down from there. That's a hundred-plus-year-old tree."

He moved like an inchworm backwards, but a snap cracked the silence.

She caught sight of him a half second before he hit the ground with a loud bam. The phone rang, but she abandoned it to rush to his side. "Are you hurt?"

"Only my pride." Drew brushed off his pants and shirt before he twisted his arms and checked his legs.

The phone kept ringing in her ear. "You hurt more than that. The limb you just broke was the one that the owner's husband crawled out on to propose to her at her bedroom window when she was seventeen."

His hands cupped his head like he was keeping it from exploding.

"911, what's your emergency?"

He dropped his hands to his side. "I'll deal with this later; I'm going inside to see if I can hear it from there."

"Your coat," she shouted after him, but he trotted inside before she could get to him.

"Hello?" Gretta's voice called to her.

Carissa eyed the tree and the chimney. "Yeah, um, there's a cat, and we think it's stuck in the chimney."

"Can you hear it crying?"

She cupped her ear in hopes of hearing something. "We could, but it's not making any sounds right now."

Greta cleared her throat as if she'd just woken up, which was probably the case. She did tend to nap in between calls, which allowed a lot of napping time. "Okay, I'll send Charlie over with the big ladder."

"I'm at the inn."

"Okay, hang tight. Charlie is over in Creekside, so it might take an hour or two."

An uneasiness twisted her stomach. "That long? It's awful cold out. Will it survive that long?"

"There's a chance. To be honest, if it stopped crying, it's probably too late already."

Her chest ached. Poor little creature. "I'll see if we can get a ladder."

"No, don't do that. We don't want to have to rescue you, Carissa." Several beeps sounded in the background. "Got to run. Wait for Charlie."

Carissa clutched Drew's coat to her chest, catching a whiff of fresh clean manly aroma with a hint of expensive aftershave on the collar. She shuffled up the front steps, snagged his bag and the boxes, and went inside to deliver the bad news but found Drew covered in soot, coughing and spitting. A dark cloud of ash exploded in the air around him. Mrs. Graysman was going to have a coronary when she saw her area rug covered in black. "What are you doing?"

He wiped his eyes with his dark sleeve, only smearing more dirt over his face, making him look like a Burglar Santa Claus. "She's alive." The ball of black he held high and proud in front of him looked like a piece of charcoal.

Mew. Mew. Okay, a meowing piece of charcoal, but that little sound melted her fear and warmed her heart. Of course, Drew's white teeth and eyes shining from behind the darkness were wide, as if he'd saved the town from flooding. If he only knew the trouble he'd be in when Mrs. Graysman saw this, not to mention the tree outside. She didn't have the heart to tell him, not when she knew how much he hated to be unkempt. And boy, he was unkempt at the moment.

Drew snuggled the little thing under his chin, making it look like he had an old coal mining beard. The large-framed, militant man who strived for perfection had never looked so good. The way he cuddled the tiny creature in his hands and analyzed its face and paws made him resemble the hunk-holding-a-baby poster. The one that made all women swoon. Not Carissa. She never got it.

Until now.

CHAPTER NINE

GRITTY, itchy dust clung to Drew's teeth, eyelashes, skin, clothes, everything. He hated it, but he hated seeing the poor little kitten suffer more. People were unpredictable and emotionally messy, but animals were solid. You knew what they needed and wanted in life. "Can you get some water and a towel? This baby isn't going to like this, but we need to clean her up to make sure she doesn't have any lacerations."

Carissa stood there staring at him as if she'd seen a soot-covered ghost. "Ah, yeah, sure. Kitchen. There. Follow me." She walked with a blank stare through a swinging door holding his coat to her chest.

He kicked off his shoes in an attempt not to put prints through the beautiful old home. Sounds above stirred, but no one came down to see what was going on. No one to help. "Maybe we should take her to the vet." He entered the large, cabinet-lined kitchen with marble countertops and found Carissa standing next to a stainless-steel farm sink. His coat rested on the back of a dining chair and the boxes on the island.

"There's a vet, but she's probably out doing her farm runs. I can leave her a message to come check out the kitten after she returns to town." Carissa stepped away from the sink and dialed her phone. "Hey, cancel the fire department call."

He held the squirming kitten over the sink and brushed as much soot off its fur as possible.

"Yep, cat is out." She opened a drawer and removed a few dishtowels and set them on the counter. "No, I didn't play hero. It was Drew Lancaster. He saved the cat."

The poor little thing squirmed and screamed but didn't appear to be cut or harmed in anyway, only dirty and tiny. "Sorry, little one. You aren't going to like this." He checked the water temperature and then shoved the stopper into the sink.

"Can you radio Dr. Mauldin and let her know to stop by to check the animal out when she returns to town? Okay, great. I better go help bathe the cat. That's right…bathe." She snickered and then hung up the phone.

"Here, let me hold it while you wash your face. You can use one of those towels." She slid her fingers over his and gently retrieved the little fur puff. It was cozy and warm in the kitchen, and he had to admit it was calming to be in a place where you didn't hear yelling through walls and honks on the street, not to mention the music they played downstairs. Maybe Lori was right and the quaint inn would be a better place to sleep than the couch at their makeshift office.

Carissa smelled nice, a mix of sweet yet spicy hometown goodness.

He found relief from the obnoxious black dust on his face with warm water and some soap. Still, only the cat would fit in the sink, not him. "I think I need more than a shower. You say there's a fire department here? They might have to hose me off."

She quirked her head to one side. "I didn't know you had a sense of humor. You wear it well."

Was that a compliment? Wow, maybe he was on to something. Lori would be happy. He decided he better just keep his mouth shut, though. If he opened it again, he might ruin the moment and damage any progress he'd unintentionally made.

Carissa held the kitten like a newborn baby, leaving black marks on her sweater. For the first time, he didn't mind the mess. It looked good on her, holding the little cuddly creature. She'd been a defensive, walls up, at a distance kind of person until this moment.

He finished cleaning his face and hands and then retrieved the kitten, holding it up to look eye to eye with it. "What are we going to call you?"

"Midnight," she suggested but didn't sound convinced.

He dipped the squirming kitten into the water, and darkness pooled in the water. After a few rubs and dunks, cries and hisses, they realized it wasn't a black cat at all. "I think we should call her something else, huh?"

"Yeah, no doubt." Carissa covered the kitten's eyes and poured some more water over her.

"She looks like a little rat right now, but we don't want to call her that." He used a drop of dish soap and finished the job and then held the kitten up to Carissa's awaiting opened towel. He wrapped the towel around its little body and rubbed it dry. When he removed the towel, it looked like a puffy cotton ball.

"Wow, that makes a difference." Carissa scratched the kitten's head. "You're a little cutie, huh?"

"She sure is." He realized he said that while looking at Carissa, and she noticed. They were standing close, so close he noticed a wayward yellow speck in her eyes, but it didn't look out of place. It was more of a highlight mark to the blue.

"Snowball. How about Snowball?"

"Cute, and she looks like one," he agreed but not sure it fit the squirming little thing perfectly.

"What's going on?" a woman's voice screeched from the living room. He recognized it as Mrs. Graysman, the owner of the inn. He'd only seen the woman the two times he'd been in the inn long enough to take a shower and to work with Lori in the parlor for an hour last night.

Drew unplugged the sink and cuddled the kitten to his chest. "I'll go face the music. Can you clean this sink and floor?"

Carissa wiped her hands and shot him the first soft I-don't-want-you-to-be-run-out-of-town look since his arrival. "You don't have to do that."

"Yes, I do. If there's one thing I am a stickler about, it's taking responsibility for one's actions. Wish me luck."

"You'll need more than luck." Carissa patted the kitten's head. "You better put on your cutest little smile to help out your hero. Mrs. Graysman is a sucker for all things small and sweet."

"I'll lead with Snowball, then." He took a deep breath and headed for the door.

"You realize if you name it, you keep it. Town law." She squatted with towel in hand so he couldn't see her face since the center island blocked his view. No way of knowing if she was pulling his unsouthernly chain or not. He'd deal with that later, though. There was no room in his life for a pet, no matter how adorable. Commitment wasn't his strongest skill.

Based on the moaning in the other room, he needed to do some damage control and quick. With a deep breath, he pushed open the door and entered the living area to find Mrs. Graysman with her tight curls and tight lips turning in the center of the room. "What happened?"

He bolted to her with his best smile that usually changed women's attitudes toward him. "I promise to clean this area, and the company will reimburse you for any damages."

"Company? I don't trust no fancy companies. Look at my rug!" She pointed to a size eleven male footprint. He glanced at his shoes only a foot away from his mark.

"I'm so sorry for the mess. This little kitten here was trapped in your fireplace. When I opened the flue to try to coax her out, all this soot erupted. The chimney must have needed cleaning for years." He chuckled, but she wasn't laughing. She glowered at him with an air of resentment. So much for his humor streak. "It covered me from head to toe. I took off my shoes so I wouldn't track it any farther, but this little one needed attention quick." He held up the little puff ball, and she eyed it, but her glower turned to a narrowed gaze, ready-to-attack expression.

"That darn cat has been hanging around my place all week. I told the council something needed to be done about the feral cats. They eat my plants in spring, cry all night, and leave poo on my front lawn. It's probably got some sort of disease. I run an inn, not an animal rescue. Get that thing out of here."

He glanced around the room, trying to find something to help his case, but he was at a loss. This could go viral on the small-town tree of shame. He was sure if Davey caught wind, he'd use this as ammo for his social execution. He needed to do something and quick. "Yes, ma'am. I'll have a cleaning crew come out within the hour, and I'll have a tree removal service haul away the branch."

Her mouth opened. The eyes wide, shock-filled face told him he'd just signed his arrest warrant. "You broke my tree?" she screeched at a decimal he didn't know was possible, and he knew his days in Sugar Maple were numbered.

CHAPTER TEN

MRS. GRAYSMAN JOLTED CARISSA into action. No matter how much she didn't want to be the center of all this business for the town, she didn't wish Mrs. Graysman's wrath on anyone. Except maybe Judas Jackie.

She snagged the plate of scones and shoved open the door. "Mrs. Graysman, I'm so happy you're here. Mr. Lancaster told me how he was going to talk to you about filming here at the inn, so I told him I would walk with him since I was delivering these. Isn't it exciting? I mean, this place screams small-town charm, doesn't it?"

Her angry snarl relaxed into a droopy grin. "He was?"

"I was?" For a bright businessman, he sure was slow.

"Of course, remember? You said you wanted to capture the heart of the town, and when you saw this place, you thought it was the perfect symbol of southern charm."

"Yes, we were hoping to do a shoot here. As soon as Ms. Donahue finishes making her special treats for us to take test shots, we'll be here. I'll have Lori set up a time with you."

"My inn? I thought it didn't make the cut. Mayor Horton, who we all know has never forgiven me for the incident of 1968, blacklisted me from the project."

"She'll have to agree if she wants this to move forward, and whatever Drew Lancaster says he needs, she has to give him." Carissa waved the plate of scones in front of her for added distraction.

"And I want this place," he said with authority.

That was the Drew Lancaster she had met in the mayor's office a few days ago.

Mrs. Graysman snagged a scone and took a bite. "Well, I like that Lori girl. She's nice. You, I haven't seen much of since you arrived. Rumor has it you slept in that old building Mayor Horton set your offices up in. What? My inn's not good enough for you?"

"It's too good. I mean, I can't wait to enjoy it tonight. I've been working past hours, so I didn't want to disturb you to unlock the front door to let me in. I guess Lori forgot to give me the key. Tonight, though, I look forward to staying here and getting a good night's sleep."

A couple entered, laughing. "Hurry. We don't want to miss the scones again."

The couple lit up at the sight of Carissa's scones, which made her day a little brighter. But they halted at the sight of the soot and Mrs. Graysman. The lady rubbed her hands together. "Sorry to interrupt. We came back from our hike early so we could enjoy one of your scones again. They are divine."

"Come in, come in. Yes, the scones are here. Please, excuse our mess. Our hero here saved this little kitten. Don't worry. A cleaning crew is coming to get this all cleaned up. In the meantime, why don't you sit in the dining room, and I'll get some fresh, warm hot chocolate for you." Mrs. Graysman snagged the plate out of Carissa's hands and grumbled low enough so only Drew and Carissa could hear. "Get this taken care of now."

The woman tugged her husband toward the stairs. "Come on. Let's go get cleaned up and hurry back before they're all gone."

"Sure thing. We're on it." Carissa let out a long breath, but when she saw the mess, she didn't feel the relief. "You said a cleaning crew. You have one in mind?"

"I was hoping you knew someone." He held Snowball to his cheek and offered his own kitten eyes.

"Fine, I'll make a call, but it'll cost you." Carissa retrieved her phone from her pocket and texted Stella, who had friends who cleaned houses. "Okay, good thing there are plenty of scones for Mrs. Graysman's two guests. But I think I'll make a peace offering dessert for them tonight for after dinner."

She shoved the box he'd abandoned on the front porch into his chest. "We best get these delivered while they are still fresh if you want to get everyone on board and welcome this project to the town. Is the project already approved for the town by the mayor? Technically yes, but without the town behind it, things can be difficult."

"But I still don't understand how baked goods are going to win the town over so that I can get this filming underway." He set the kitten down on the sofa to put his coat on. "I thought I'd just won over Mrs. Graysman." With a pinched face, he buttoned up his coat and stood as if the sleeves were lined with nails. "Great. Now I have to get this cleaned, too."

"You did, but there are more in this town than her who don't trust you."

"Do you trust me?"

She didn't know how to answer that. In an odd way she did. The man was manipulative but predictable. He didn't lie, but he did talk circles around people to get what he wanted. It was more of a gray area.

"Never mind. Just tell me once we deliver these bars that the town will be won over and we can get to work on the test shots."

"It's going to take more than one box of sweets." She retrieved

Snowball, who was hanging off the back of the sofa by her claws and thrust her at him.

He collapsed onto the cushion and put his head back on the wall. "I don't have time for this."

"You're going to have to make time." She scanned the room, trying to think of a way to make this man understand the town better.

The scent of pine trees still filled the air, even though the massive Christmas tree had been removed a few days ago. It had been beautiful and filled the room with cheer. She spotted the album on the coffee table and sat down on the couch next to him. "Here, look at this."

Snowball climbed up his coat and around his neck to settle under his chin.

"It's the Christmas album that's left out all year. Mrs. Graysman takes photos and places them in here. It's been done every year since the first Christmas that this home became an inn a hundred years ago." She opened the front cover, and he scooted closer to see, his side touching her arm. "Wow, that looks old."

"As I said, tradition. Something that's important to the people of Sugar Maple, Tennessee. Here." She flipped to the last page, where she could show him the goings on only a few weeks ago. "This is where the preschoolers made decorations for the tree, and here's where the elders lit the tree—oh, and here's where the mayor read *The Little Drummer Boy* to the guests of the inn."

"They do the town celebrations in this inn for the holidays?" he asked.

"Well, no, not all of them. We do many events in the square. This is just one part of this town's Christmas, but each part is important to us."

He nodded and flipped through some of the pages. "I see that Sugar Maple celebrates Christmas, but this is a new year. How am I interrupting anything now?"

Footsteps sounded overhead, reminding her they weren't

alone. "It doesn't. I'm trying to explain that waltzing into a town family and interrupting things without even so much as a hello and a host or hostess gift is rude here in the south."

The front door opened, sending a breeze into the warm parlor. Drew shot up as if standing at attention when he saw that it was Ms. Horton. She stopped in the entryway and gave Carissa an inquisitive eyebrow raise. "I heard about the catastrophe here, but I didn't know it was this bad."

Busted. Carissa needed to do some damage control and quick. "He's a town hero. Saved the cat, and he helped make a special treat for the elders. He's going to personally deliver them, but I was running late and needed to drop these first."

Ms. Horton removed her gloves. "I see. Mr. Lancaster, I hope you're enjoying your stay here."

"Yes, this town is…exceptional," he said with a grit to his tone.

Carissa knew what he meant by that, and based on Ms. Horton's twist of her lips, she knew too. The gig was up. Carissa would have to stop dancing around things and commit to this project, even if her heart wasn't in it.

"Would you excuse us for a moment? I need to steal our girl for something in the dining room."

"Of course." Drew returned to the photo album without protest. "Actually, this is perfect. I'll go clean up before we head out. Give me ten minutes." He shot up the stairs, leaving Carissa to face Ms. Horton.

"Young lady, what game are you playing at?"

"The same one you are." Carissa nudged the plate of scones toward Ms. Horton, hoping to distract her.

"What are you talking about?" Ms. Horton snagged a scone.

Carissa took advantage of Ms. Horton's mouth being full and hit straight on with the facts. "Please. You stuck the production people's offices in Mark's former apartment above his family's old store. Just to make a point that I should move on with my life."

"I put their offices up there because they would meet more townspeople if they worked in the square opposed to being tucked away in the inn all the time. But what about you? What kind of stunt is this?"

"It wasn't a stunt. It happened, but he needs to understand that if he messes with us, he is going to deal with the consequences. If you don't like how I'm handling him, you should push for Jackie's segment to be the big spotlight business. We all know she's the one who wants it the most and would do anything to get her day on television, or internet, or whatever this thing is."

"That's exactly why you're the only one for this job. The only person who can make this work for the town." Her cheeks tightened and her forehead wrinkled with a pensive expression.

"Why me? The one who doesn't want to do it?"

"Jackie would mess it up by being a diva. Mary-Beth's too out there—she'd try to turn it into some yoga coffee show or something. She's amazing when you need someone to think outside the box, but not this."

"Then give it to Stella. That's who needs it and deserves it the most."

"She'll be second. You need to be first. Do I even need to mention how this would end before it ever began with abrasive Stella? And before you ask about Felicia, don't. She's the mediator for everything. The person who would negotiate and give them whatever they want. Not you. You'll handle this with the sweet disposition you've always had, the dignity of a southern lady, and with the intelligence God gave you."

Carissa wanted to argue, wanted to beg to be left out of all of this, but she couldn't let the people down who had taken care of her after her parents left for bigger and better lives. "Fine, but if I can get Drew to work with Jackie instead, you have to accept that. And no more trying to mend that friendship. It's dead and gone."

Ms. Horton opened her mouth, and Carissa knew she was

going to try to convince her to fix things with Jackie, but instead she popped her last bit of scone into her mouth.

No answer was better than an all-out argument that Ms. Horton would win.

She flicked a wayward crumb from her vest and headed for the door. "I need to get to a meeting. I'll catch you later, darlin'." She paused at the end of the table. "Remember, we're all counting on you to make this work. You wouldn't want our town to have to break up because we can't keep our businesses open."

Carissa wanted to tell Ms. Horton that wasn't fair, but that didn't matter. It was the truth. The town had been struggling for so long that if something wasn't done, more businesses would have to close. Stella would be the first to go, and Carissa couldn't let that happen. Not even if it meant that she had to publicly humiliate herself in front of the world...and Jackie.

CHAPTER ELEVEN

DREW AND CARISSA walked in silence through the sleet. An uneasiness settled between them, and he didn't like it. He liked it even less than the feeling of soot smeared over his skin. For some reason he cared. Probably because she'd saved him from Mrs. Graysman when she'd seen the damage he'd caused. He'd found more trouble in a few days in this small town than Knox found in a nightclub over a weeklong party in Miami.

"When you get inside, don't say anything. Set the box of treats on the table, open the lid, and then stay out of the way."

The kitten purred underneath his jacket close to his chest. "You make it sound like I'm making an offering to some tribal god."

"Ha. It kind of does sound like that." She tightened her scarf around her neck and eyed the fashion store down the street. The one Jacqueline probably owned.

"I'll make the offering with no deviation." He adjusted his camera bag strap on his shoulder that kept sliding down with the snow melting on his clothes. "I don't want to get any more of the town on my bad side."

She bit her bottom lip in a way that told him she was keeping her words inside, so he stopped at the lightpost in front of a sewing store. "Tell me. Did I do something wrong beyond breaking a historical tree and destroying the carpet inside the Victorian home that sits as a symbol of small-town charm?"

To his relief, his words provoked a release of her bottom lip, allowing the rosebud color to flood through it again. "No. It's not that. It's just... I want you to consider what I proposed." She leaned against the light pole, shivering. "Trust me when I tell you that Jacqueline is the perfect person for this show. She'll win over every man with her looks and charisma, and all the women will want to be her. It's a win-win."

"If I was trying to sell dresses and a personality, sure." He noticed the way her gaze connected with the ground and realized what the real problem was. The beautiful, sweet, energetic, talented woman in front of him didn't believe she was good enough for the job. "You know you're perfect. For this spotlight, I mean. The only one in this town I've met so far who I would want to work with on this project."

"You're saying that because you want me to hurry up and make the perfect product for your test shots so you can get out of here before you find yourself being sacrificed." Carissa's lips curled into a half smile.

"You got me." The kitten poked her fuzzy little head out as if to see why he'd stopped walking but then buried herself back into his jacket for the warmth.

"I almost believe you. How can I doubt a man who breaks tree limbs and nearly his neck trying to save a little animal?"

"Ah, shucks, it was nothing, ma'am."

Carissa burst out laughing. "This isn't the Old West, and you're not John Wayne. Don't try that on Davey."

The guilt halted his steps and he faced her, looking at her for the first time beyond a job he had to handle. "I appreciate your help, and as a thank-you, I'll talk to Knox and see if I can persuade him to focus on the dress shop angle first. Perhaps I can even sell the knitting store over the bakery. No promises. I don't want to get your hopes up, but I'll do my best."

Her eyes softened, jaw softened...and his heart softened.

The wind whistled in between the buildings, sending a chill through the air, but when she stepped closer to him, it was as if a bubble of heat surrounded him. "Thank you. If you can convince the powers that be to focus on another business, I'll do everything I can to help you win over the town."

He stepped into her personal space, but this time she didn't back away from him. "Why don't you want the world to see you?"

The happiness gleaming around her dulled. "It's complicated. That's an over-lunch conversation, not a standing-on-the-sidewalk talk."

"Sorry. I didn't mean to pry." He scanned the storefronts, looking for something else to say to end the awkward moment.

"You city boys really are slow, aren't you?" She brushed past him and headed for the stairs.

"What are you talking about?" he asked, feeling like he'd entered the conversation a minute too late to follow it.

"I just gave you an in. That lunch date you've been begging for, you know?"

He chuckled. "Begging is a strong word."

"Maybe, but not as strong as your stench." She waved her hand in front of her nose. "I think that kitten must've added a new cologne to your jacket."

"Great. I guess I'll need to go and change again before our date."

"Nondate, business luncheon. And you're not getting out of this that easily. She touched his arm but then stepped away with a mischievous tilt to her head. She stood on her toes and messed his hair, tugged his scarf so it was loose. "There, you look perfect."

The way her eyes and tone dipped lodged a lump in his throat that he had to force down before he could speak again. "For a firing squad at the recreation center?"

"First of all, it isn't a recreation center. It's the former business and apartment from my ex's family."

"As Lori would say...ah, awkward." He shifted between feet and eyed the building. "Does it bother you that I'm up there working in his old place?"

"I thought it would, but it doesn't. Seeing it being used has actually helped me move forward. Don't tell Ms. Horton that, though." She took his arm. "Now stop stalling. Come on."

Nerves chiseled at his resolve to enter the building. He hadn't been this apprehensive since he had to breach a compound during his service days. At least most of the time he knew who was friend and who was foe. Not here. "What do I do once I put these on the table and open the box?"

"Stand out of the way and focus on Snowball. The women will flock to you with that big ball of cuteness."

"Thanks. I didn't know that you found me adorable. Good to know." He winked, trying to keep the mood light and happy, because when Carissa smiled, she lit up the gloomy winter day.

"Don't even try it, Mr. Party Planner. You know I meant the cat."

"Okay, baker." He reached for the door at the same time she did, covering her hand with his. If he didn't have his glove on, he could imagine how soft and warm her hand would be, but he did have his glove on, and he shouldn't have those thoughts.

"And don't look so frightened," she said and then turned the knob and opened the door into the geriatric gang ghetto.

"Here goes nothing, Snowball," he whispered to the little girl in his coat and then headed inside behind Carissa, glad to have the human shield to Davey at first entrance.

Before the glowers could turn to words or physical contact, Drew set the box on the table, opened it, and backed away. Despite wanting to stay warm, he removed his coat so the ladies could see Snowball. Carissa was right… There was a smelly wet spot on his coat.

The music cut off and they approached with snarls and grunts. Davey led the charge until his nose crinkled and he stopped at the table. "Those Southern Man Bars?"

Carissa shot him a speak-you-fool look.

"Yes." Drew returned his attention to the kitten, who drew Ms. Gina over.

"Isn't that precious. Come look at this little guy." Ms. Gina lit up like she was on stage again. Her liver-spotted hand with painted coral nails patted Snowball's head. "So precious."

"This is Snowball," he announced.

"Where'd Snowball come from?" Mrs. Melba asked.

Carissa stepped into the center of the crowd. "Our local hero here saved her life. Fell out of a tree and was coated in soot, but in the end, he saved her from exposure and breaking her little neck lodged in the chimney."

"I saved a cat from a tree once," Davey said, as if his save was better than Drew's.

The women crowded around him, and based on Davey's ears doing the jig and his hands wringing, this wasn't doing Drew any favors. Then his nose twitched like a rabbit back and forth, up and down. He shifted focus to the box. "Bet he ruined them, but guess I should try them anyway. Just to judge him and his bad cooking skills."

Carissa remained silent, but a tightening of her cheeks told Drew that this was going in the right direction.

"I'm taking my life in my hands here, ladies. Look at that man all covered in grime and shame. Didn't even think about getting dirty. Even I know you don't want to open the flue of a chimney if it hasn't been used in years."

Drew wanted to open his mouth and protest that he couldn't know that it hadn't worked in years, but with the shake of Carissa's head, he knew better. So he held his breath, waiting for

Davey's response on his offering. Based on the women cooing, he'd already won them over. Well, at least Snowball had.

"You should take her with you as a pet." He held Snowball out to Ms. Gina.

"Can't. They got rules against that," Davey announced with a judge's authority. "They're always making up stuff to make our life miserable. But in this case, I agree. That little thing would cause us all to have allergies and fleas come spring." He shoved a bar into his mouth, and his face stretched until there were few wrinkles left. His eyes were wide and his lips smacked. Then he spotted Drew watching him and smashed his face together again. "Ain't bad."

That caught Mrs. Malter's attention, and she shuffled over there with her walker. "Let me try one."

Ms. Gina remained with the furry friend she'd made, but her hand kept missing the cat and petting his chest. Something told him she did that on purpose, but he kept his trap shut. The things he'd been forced to do today... They didn't pay him enough for this, yet he stayed. Out of duty, honor, or stupidity, he wasn't sure.

"These are the best ever. Tell us the truth. Carissa made these," Ms. Gina accused.

Carissa grabbed a bar of her own. "Let me taste this. No way this outsider can bake as well as me. I just told him what ingredients I used, and then he added to that." She took a dramatic bite and cooed and exclaimed and then tossed it down. "He does know how to bake. Well, I guess I'm not needed around here."

Davey put his arm around her. "They ain't that good. You're the best baker ever. He just got lucky. I'm sure he stole your recipe or something." The man grabbed two more bars. "He'll have to prove himself more than this."

Prove himself? How much more did these people want from him?

"He'll have to bake something for the next town hall meeting.

Guess we'll see then if he's to be trusted. Or if he's a lying, thieving, recipe-stealing outsider."

Carissa swished through the room, grabbed Drew by the arm, and shoved him toward the door. "You did it. You won Davey over," she whispered.

He wasn't sure he'd done that, but he did want to finally get this project moving. "Here, you take Snowball. I'll return to the bakery tomorrow, and we can figure out a real plan to work together on this."

"Oh no, you don't. That isn't my kitten. Besides, I sent a text for the vet to come here, and no pets are allowed in the bakery. It's against code."

"But this little girl is going to shed all over everything. Besides, it needs to stay here in town when I leave. This is her home."

Carissa ignored him and raced out of the building, leaving him holding the cat, watching Davey who looked like he swallowed the canary. He stormed upstairs to Lori, who sat on the couch with her feet up and the heat blasting again.

"You. I blame you." He set the cat on her chest and held his hands out to the radiator. His fingers were stiff from the cold and took a second to uncurl.

"What happened to you? Or a better question, what did you do now?"

"I listened to you. Now I own a cat, I'm working with a woman who doesn't want to do the show, and I baked. That's right. I baked. And look at me. My hair is a mess, a cat went on me, and my shoes are still covered in ash, all because I listened to my assistant when she told me to play nice with others. Look what nice does to a person."

She doubled over, laughing hysterically.

"This isn't funny. I'm no closer to having test shots and the perfect set and product. I've got a call with Knox that I keep putting off, but I have nothing to tell him."

"I think you have plenty to tell him." She snickered. "You tell him that you're the new town hero, which means you've won the town's approval."

"How do you know all this?" he asked, eyeing Lori holding the cat wrong. After it rolled off her body and she had to catch it midair before it hit the floor, he decided to take Snowball back.

"Thin walls." She sat up and pointed to her cell phone. "And Mayor Horton called. Apparently Knox sent an attorney to her office this morning and demanded the contract be signed by the end of today or the deal's off. He's tired of the small-town politics and didn't like the mayor telling him this project was a go and then not returning the contracts yet. You have a couple of hours to convince Carissa to tell the town that this project is a definite go, or by the end of the day, you'll be fired."

CHAPTER TWELVE

THE AFTERNOON INVITED the sun out to warm the air and made for a pleasant walk over to Maple Table, where Carissa found Drew seated with his laptop and folders in front of him.

Her heart slowed at the realization that this was a business lunch. For some reason, she'd convinced herself that Drew Lancaster enjoyed her company as more than a business relationship. Perhaps her dating meter needed to be adjusted after all these years.

The front door chimed over her head. Heat blasted her as if she'd entered a furnace instead of a restaurant. "Hey, Doris. Think you can turn down the heat a little?"

She laughed. "Broken again. Sorry. I've got Mickey coming now."

Carissa uncurled her scarf from around her neck and shoved it in her oversized bag full of junk and headed for Drew standing next to the table with arms open. Maybe it was a date.

He stepped aside and pulled her chair out for her, causing her to face the fact that her overactive imagination was in super mode. The kitten popped her head up out of his bag, and he quickly shooed it back inside. "Shh. You agreed to stay out of sight."

She slid into her chair and pointed at all the stuff on the table. "What's all this?"

"I know I promised to convince Knox to focus on Jacqueline's business, but I already had this proposal together for you, so I thought I'd share it anyway. You know, just in case you come later in the project."

She browsed the images of decorated cakes and cookies and pies. All of them looked like Martha Stewart followed a 1950s Betty Crocker recipe and Vera Wang styled it. Processed. Perfect. Plastic.

"What is it? You don't like these? Remember, it has to look appealing."

"That's just it. They do, but they look, well…" She didn't know how to say what she was thinking without being rude.

Drew studied the photos as if to uncover what she saw. "Tell me. It's okay."

"They look fake. Yes, it's something that looks visually appealing, but I don't want to eat it. I see food designed to fool the viewer. It's like a perfect faux apple—shiny, lifeless, too…corporate. It doesn't have any character like you'd have in a small town. We offer a welcome home kind of flavor here. Not a stuffy, five star, you're-scared-to-eat-it-because-it's-too-pretty kind of food.

"People don't want to see flaws. They want perfection. We want people to see it and fall in love with it so much they want to make it. They want to know about the recipe. About the person who made it. The tips and tricks and secrets."

Carissa slid into the seat and set her bag and coat in the chair next to her. "I don't have any secrets. We live in a small town. Sometimes I wish I did, though. It would make life easier."

Doris plopped Carissa's usual in front of her, a Rueben on sourdough bread. "Davey told me you eat salads, so I brought you one. Let me know if you want anything else."

"As I said, no secrets." Carissa picked up her silverware and set the napkin in her lap. "So is Knox a firm no about focusing the first show on Jacqueline?"

"Actually, he told me to do a joint program test. Have you two in dresses she made holding desserts that you made."

The heater felt like it had been set to a tropical setting, sending beads of perspiration down the back of her neck. "No. That won't work."

"You can't set aside your hate for Jacqueline long enough to work together?" He asked a difficult question in a simple tone.

Carissa let out a long breath and studied the chip in the edge of the Formica table. "Hate is a strong word, but you're close. I don't trust her, and she's a challenge to see on a day-to-day basis, but I don't have a choice."

"I'm sorry for whatever happened between you two. It's obvious that even now you're still troubled by it."

"You deserve to know what you're getting into and why I won't work with her." She smoothed out the napkin in her lap and picked up a fork as if her stomach wasn't churning so much she wouldn't dare take a bite. "She ran off with my fiancé the night he proposed to me," she said, as if reading off town hall meeting minutes.

"She what?" His shoulders stiffened. "That's awful."

She shrugged. "It's in the past. The guy is out of our lives forever, and as Ms. Horton said, she did me a favor. Unfortunately, the side effect of betrayal is no trust. She demolished that, and even now, I don't trust that she won't do something to hurt me again. It doesn't have to be a romantic betrayal. It could be something during this project. You see, I can't work with her, so you better sell Knox on just having her do the segment. Perhaps after that I'll figure something out so that I can create something we both love and is appropriate for Knox's fans."

He picked up his fork but didn't dig into his food. "You think the waitress would be offended if I wanted to change to what you're eating?"

"I thought you were a salad man."

"Nope." He shoved the images in his bag and raised his hand. "I don't like garlic or anchovies, but yours looks delicious." He lowered his hand. "Unless I'm going to turn her against me if I don't eat this? I don't want to have to face any more enemies in this town."

"It's fine. She won't." Carissa took a bite of her sandwich while Drew exchanged his food.

People watched his every move, and she knew they were assessing his intent and trustworthiness. "You should work in the community more instead of hiding in that apartment. Besides, you'll be more comfortable at the Maple Grounds than in that drafty old apartment."

"That sounds like a good idea." He scratched his cheek and swished his lips. "You know, this is a problem. You don't want to bake, and you don't want to work with Jacqueline, but Knox wants you or at the minimum you and Jacqueline."

Snowball hopped out of the bag and onto his lap and pawed at his plate. He scooped her up and put her back in the bag.

"You'll have to keep working on him. Jacqueline's the right choice. Despite how I feel about her, she is the best person for this job. She's charismatic, beautiful, talented, and works a camera like a fashion model. Her dresses will photograph well, too. If Knox wants a win, that's what he should start with."

"I'm surprised that you'd speak of her so highly after what she put you through."

She wasn't hungry at the moment, so she set her sandwich back on her plate. "Yes, well, the town needs this or I don't think I'd be screaming her praises. For now, tell your boss she's the right choice. It'll be great."

"That look on your face says something different, but if this is what you really want, then I'll try one more time."

"Thank you."

The kitten leapt out of the bag and landed on the table, grabbed a piece of corned beef, and took off. Drew lunged from the table and chased her. "Come back here, you little stinker."

"What is that thing doing in my restaurant!" Doris turned in her orthopedic brown shoes and headed back for the kitchen. "I'll package this to go. No pets allowed inside."

Drew ducked under a table and climbed between two people, who jolted and hollered at him. "What about service pets?"

"I doubt that puff of fur is a service pet."

Drew managed to land hard on his knees near the door and snag the cat with the meat still hanging from her mouth. "It's my stress-relieving pet."

"If that thing is meant to relieve stress, you better get your money back." She shook her head and mumbled, "Darn city people always trying to pull something. Be nice to him. Listen to him. Win him over, Mayor Horton said." Doris retrieved a box from behind the counter and dumped his food unceremoniously inside and shut it. "Maybe it's time for a new mayor."

Carissa hopped up and handed her plate to Doris, who promptly dumped it into another box. "Don't worry. I'll get him out of here." She slipped on her coat, snagged Drew's bag, her stuff, and the two boxes of food. "Come on, Cat Whisperer. We better go."

Drew retrieved his jacket from her and followed her out the door, all while struggling to keep the kitten in his arms. "Sorry, I thought she'd behave. How did she manage to get out and across the room so fast?"

"She's a cat and there was food." Carissa handed him his box of food. "I have to admit that was the most entertaining and adventurous undate lunch I've ever had."

"Undate?" He quirked an eyebrow at her. "Is that a thing?"

"It is now." She welcomed the cool air with the sunshine. "We won't have many days like this in the near future. Why don't we make the most of it and give Rocky kitty here a chance to run around a bit?"

"Rocky? What happened to Snowball?" he asked while fighting the kitten, who had both paws up, slapping at him.

"Snowball is too sweet for that cat. It's all ears and keeps its paws up, ready to fight all the time. An underdog who had to battle for its win. Rocky."

"Rocky is a boy's name. This is a sweet little girl." Drew held her up, and she smacked his nose, drawing a line of blood with her claws. "Ouch!"

"You were saying?"

"We'll go with Roxy." He stuffed her in his coat and eyed the town square. "How about over there?"

She laughed. "Always planning and manipulating for your project, I see."

"What?" He acted innocent, but she knew his choice was strategic.

"Fine, we'll sit where the entire town can see us eating lunch together. If you want them to think our undate is a date, go for it. I don't care. At least they'll talk about the new man in my life instead of the bum who got away."

"I still can't believe she did that." He crossed the street, bumping into her side as if to nudge her into believing she deserved better in life than a man-stealing ex-friend.

"She did." For once the admission didn't sting like a lashing, more like a kitten scratch. "Mary-Beth and Felicia tell me that I should thank Jaqueline for keeping me from a horrible mistake. And that I should be happy because I would've never opened my own bakery and discovered who I am and what I wanted to do with my life."

"Let me guess… Stella disagrees."

"No, she agrees with them. In her words, I escaped a life sentence with a rusty old wrench, but that doesn't mean I have to be nice to the person who sold it to me."

"Colorful."

"That's Stella." Carissa retrieved her scarf from her bag and laid it on the ground. "Here, sit on this. The ground is still a little damp."

"I don't want to ruin your scarf."

"No worries. I'm a wash and wear kind of girl."

"So I've noticed." Drew sat cross-legged with the cat in his lap, but she didn't stay. "It's refreshing." Roxy climbed up his thigh and darted around in circles chasing nonexistent things in the air and then skittered up a short tree nearby.

"I won't apologize for being me. Glitter and glamor are not my thing, and that's why you belong with Jacqueline."

"I'm not convinced Jacqueline's the right girl for me."

"For you?"

"For the project, I mean." Drew retrieved the cat from the tree before it made it too high for him to reach and settled back down. "I'm still hoping you'll change your mind."

"Why's that?"

"Because I think you're right."

"About what?"

"About those photos I pulled to show you. They're rehearsed and overdone with no character, but you have character. We only need to figure out how to dress it up enough for people to want to look deeper to find what lies below the surface. That will be the winning content for this project. And I believe you're the only one who could make that happen. You, Carissa Donahue, are unique and special, so don't ever change. Not for me, not for the town, not for Jacqueline, and especially not for a man who was too stupid to know what he had when a seductive girl walked by and distracted him. I agree with Stella... He's a rusty old wrench who doesn't deserve another thought."

Carissa opened her box to avoid acknowledging his words. How did you ignore something you didn't believe from a person you didn't trust? Then again, maybe it was time to let go of old wounds and open up to new possibilities.

CHAPTER THIRTEEN

THE AROMA of maple and coffee beans woke Drew enough for him to concentrate on his work, but the people mulling around nearby made him uneasy. He leaned over the table and whispered to Lori, "I thought southern people were all about manners."

She eyed him over the rim of the ceramic mug. "They're a friendly bunch. Why?"

"Because their parents never taught them not to stare. I'm from Los Angeles, and I know not to do that." He lifted his drink and took a sniff. "What did you order me? It smells strong yet has an almond scent."

Roxy stirred in her box at his feet, but thank goodness she didn't wake up. That cat had worn him out, climbing the curtains of his room in the inn, meowing all hours, not to mention wanting to sleep on his neck.

She tapped her ring against the side of her cup. "I didn't get a chance. Mary-Beth, the owner, prides herself in knowing what her patrons want. She said she created that uniquely for your tastes."

"How would she know my tastes?"

"I'm not sure, but she nailed mine. Light roast, with a hint of peppermint and chocolate without being sweet." She held a hand to the side of her lips. "Maybe they're aliens."

He laughed and took a tentative sip of his own beverage. It wasn't just good. It was as if he'd been put on a cloud with warm sunshine coating his skin and a hint of mystery. "She nailed it, all right. Dark roast but creamy and smooth with a hint of almond. Not enough to take away from the coffee bean, but perfectly balanced so it doesn't taste fake." He blinked and eyed the pictures in front of him. "I see it."

"See what?" Lori studied the images he palmed and moved around the table.

"The photos do look lifeless. Like drinking regular coffee out of a paper cup with a fancy swirl in the milk."

"You lost me." Lori slid a photo of a wedding cake over and studied it. "I don't see it."

An excitement seeped into him he hadn't felt in a long time. That *aha* moment when things become clear. "See this mug?"

"It's in front of me, so I should be able to see it. Is this a trick question?" Lori's eyebrows pulled together.

"Just stay with me. This mug makes drinking this coffee more of an experience than a necessity. Think about it. We go to the same corporate coffee shop on the corner each day. It has a leaf or a heart designed in the top of the drink, but we put a plastic lid over that anyway."

"Okay."

"Then we race to a meeting while sipping it, and we never even notice the flavor, except if it's too strong or too weak for us."

"I'll agree with that." Lori studied the mug in front of her as if reading the coffee beans. "The ceramic cup does make for more of a drinking experience than a necessity."

"Right, and then the flavor... It's on an entirely different universe than our normal cup of joe, right?"

"I can't argue with that."

He eyed the drink. "But there isn't a design in the top, so it isn't pretty, yet it's perfect. It has character."

Lori sat back and crossed her arms over her chest. "Okay, now I know these people are aliens and they took the real Drew Lancaster and left this deep-thinking, softer guy behind."

"Funny. Seriously, do you get what I mean? Everyone takes photos of the leaf or the heart, and we all smile at the cute design, but it doesn't make you believe that coffee tastes better than another one."

"I guess not. You do have a point. Marketing wise, though, it seems to work."

"Does it?" He held tight to the cup, warming his hands and considering the way he could photograph it to make others see what he saw and tasted and felt when he drank his coffee. "Or are they selling a decorated cup of coffee that promises to wake you up, not that it's better than any other cup of coffee?"

Lori pressed her lips together, making them almost disappear the way she did when she was thinking. "I kind of see what you mean, but if it isn't visually appealing, then how will people see that they want it? You taught me that."

"Right, but what if we made this cup of coffee look like how it tastes?"

"How do we do that?"

"I don't know." He tapped his finger against the photo of the cake with flowers on top that looked like every other cake he'd seen. "We show what it tastes like. Show the ceramic cup on a cloud with an almond drawn in the frothed milk and perhaps on yours we have peppermint shavings with a chocolate slice resting on the side like a lemon on sweet tea. And Santa is holding it."

"But you've always said to make the setting simple so that the product is the highlight."

"Yes, but perhaps we blur Santa and highlight the cup. We come up with a caption for it, like...individual flavor for the unique consumer. Not good, but something like that."

Lori shook her head. "I like what you're saying, but I'm not sure it would work, especially with Knox. You're talking about a massive campaign to educated readers and viewers."

"Do you know that sign we saw in Georgia? The one with the cows drawing about chickens? That was brilliant. I want to do something like that for this small town. If we're going to promise them that this special will change their economic outlook, then shouldn't we do something that is tailored to this town?"

"This all sounds good, but I thought you were supposed to focus on coming up with a killer segment about Jacqueline's clothing store. It's the only option after the fiasco with the auto shop segment, and Knox says coffeehouses are overdone, and it's the wrong time of year to do the nursery segment. If you keep your promise to Carissa, then this is a no starter anyway. Sure, if we do a joint segment, you could incorporate some of these ideas, but you know Jacqueline will upstage Carissa. Once Knox sees the test shots, he'll have no choice but to use Jacqueline first while we work out the kinks on Carissa."

The coffee machine roared, sending steam to the ceiling. The door chime rang, announcing new patrons.

"Maybe you're right. I don't want to force Carissa into doing the segment if she doesn't want to. That being said, she could be brilliant, captivating, the right choice." He took another sip of his coffee. "It's a shame, since we both know that first segment will be the one that draws in the most success."

"Hello, Mr. Lancaster. It's a pleasure to see you again." Jacqueline's unmistakable Marylyn Monroe tone glided into their conversation. "I'm excited that I'll be working with you. I'm sure we'll make a great team." She leaned into him so her hip pushed against his shoulder.

This woman was ruthless, and he didn't like her for what she'd done to Carissa, but he needed her if this would all work out. "Yes, Ms. Ramor. It's true. Carissa has stated that you would be perfect for this segment, so I've proposed it to Knox and he agreed to do a test shot with both of you. He wants to see if combining two business would give the segment some extra traction."

"Both of us?" She flipped her hair over her shoulder and pulled out the chair next to him. Perched on the edge, she rested her elbow on the table and toyed with her earlobe. "I really don't think that's wise. I mean, let's face it, Carissa doesn't have any experience. I was in theater in New York, and I've worked the runway, as well as being a designer."

Lori cleared her throat, as if to be announced as a person who should join the conversation, but Jacqueline couldn't be bothered with her.

"As much as I appreciate your enthusiasm for the project, Lori, my partner here, could provide more insight." He scooted his chair a foot away and snagged Roxy, who'd managed to wake up and crawl out of her bed.

Jaqueline didn't appear to like where the conversation was going, based on her sliding back in the chair and holding her purse to her chest. Funny how she changed her entire posture to face a woman. Is that how she'd won over Carissa's ex? The man had to be a fool to fall for this routine.

"Ms. Lori, I assure you that I am the right person for Knox." Jacqueline didn't even look at Lori. Instead, she eyed the cat and pressed a finger to her nose.

"You mean for Knox's segment?" Lori asked with a librarian stare.

"Right." Jacqueline shifted and rested the strap of her purse on the crook of her arm. "Trust me when I say Carissa is not organized enough for this opportunity. On the other hand, I've already brought designs, images that will be perfect for test shots."

"I handle the test shots." Drew heard the militaristic tone in his voice he thought he'd lost years ago.

"Here, I'll show you." She opened her bag and retrieved a

tablet. Her brightly colored nails tapped a code in, and the screen illuminated with fancy dresses on thin girls who looked like runway models in New York City. "As you can see, these are perfect."

Drew tugged Roxy's nails out of his skin and set her on his lap again. "They're good, but—"

"Great, so you'll call Knox and tell him you'll be doing the segment on my fashion line."

"No," Drew said with no further explanation. That's when Lori chimed in to help.

"As Mr. Lancaster mentioned, Knox has a strong position on this, so we'll need to get some test shots with you both. Your best option is to make sure that you're the one who stands out in the test shots. With two of you, he might decide to do a program with both or one of you. We won't know until we do the shoot in a few days."

Jacqueline's eyes glimmered with what could only be described as a sailor disembarking for shore leave after a year at sea. "This sounds perfect. I'll get to work. If I know Carissa, she won't even have anything to photograph by then. Don't get me wrong. She is a sweet, small-town girl who can bake, but she wouldn't even have a store if it wasn't for Stella. The girl is too disorganized."

"They say the disorganized types are actually creative geniuses." Drew looked down his own nose at her, and this time she took the hint.

Roxy raised a paw and hissed at Jacqueline, forcing her to lean away from them.

"I look forward to our photo shoot. Please send me time and place. If you hand me your phone, I can put my number in it for you."

Lori chuckled. That was the first time Drew ever heard her less than professional with a client. "I assure you that we're organized, and I already have your contact information."

"Fantastic." She clapped her hands together and twirled from her seat. How she spun in those heels was a mystery he didn't care to investigate. "Good day."

When she'd exited Maple Grounds, Drew buried himself in the aroma of his coffee. It smelled a little like the cupcake Carissa had made that reminded him of home.

"Wow," Lori said.

Drew nodded and retrieved his laptop from his bag while balancing Roxy in his other arm. "I know. She's something."

"She is, but you're the one who shocked me."

"Me?" Drew set his laptop down and opened it. "Listen, if you're going to give me grief for being rude, she had it coming. I don't like people who put others down to get ahead."

"Nope. Although, I will remind the old Drew Lancaster that this is a job and emotions are left at the door." She retrieved her own laptop. "I'm talking about the fact that binary Drew defended a girl for being disorganized."

He couldn't remember the pin to his computer, the one he'd used for six months. "As I said, I don't like people putting others down. That's all. Don't read too much into it."

"Militant Drew Lancaster who can't stand dust saved a kitten and ended up covered in soot."

He didn't like the way she smiled at him. He didn't like what she said. He didn't like the truth of it all. Thank goodness this project would be moving forward in a few days, which meant he could move on in a few weeks, leaving these crazy townspeople behind.

"I have one question." Lori didn't wait for his answer. "Are you spending so much time with Carissa, rescuing kittens and cooking for town elders, because you want to win our bet? Or because I was right and you really like her?"

CHAPTER FOURTEEN

CARISSA STRETCHED the kinks from her back, turned the sign to open, and unlocked the front door. The morning sun peered through the clouds outside, but another cold front meant that it would be gray for days.

She slipped the apron over her head and tied it at her waist. The door flew open, sending a cold breeze through the bakery.

"Good morning. Oh my goodness, I'm so glad you're open. I'm in a pickle. Can we send some people to you for warmth, coffee, and some food? Our tour bus broke down. That friendly girl across the street already took some of our clients in, but there's no more room in the coffee shop."

Carissa lit up at the thought of having some patrons. "Sure. Please invite them inside."

The woman turned and held up a flag, waving it like a call to battle. "Great. Listen, the company will pick up all expenses. Keep track, and give me the bill at the end."

"I can do that." Carissa pulled out her notepad from behind the counter.

Two older couples entered. Poor people were clinging together for warmth.

"Please, come in. You can check out what I have in the display case. There is plenty to choose from since you're here early." Who was she kidding? They could've arrived at four in the afternoon and there would still be tons left over.

A dozen people flooded in of all ages, with five more behind them. Her pulse quickened as more and more people filled the room. She'd never seen her place with wall-to-wall people. There weren't enough seats for them all.

With a deep breath, she formulated a plan. "Why don't I set out tastings at each of the tables and you can all share." She retrieved large platers from her catering closet, plated ten of them, and set them at each table. Her hand didn't even clear the area before people dug in to the food.

A young woman with two kids handed each a croissant. "Thank you so much. We're starving."

"No worries. I can have more out in less than fifteen minutes." Carissa handed them each a napkin.

"You don't know how much this means to us. We've been stuck without food since late last night."

"Oh, my. That's terrible." Carissa would give these people food for free if the touring company wasn't going to pick up the tab. "Relax and enjoy. You're welcome here as long as you would like."

Someone tapped her on her shoulder, and she turned to find Drew and Lori with bags. "What's going on? I thought we had a meeting set for eight?"

"Yes, but we'll have to reschedule. I'm so sorry." Carissa brushed past them and headed for the kitchen, waving Drew to follow. "These poor people have been stuck all night and need food." She bit her lip, trying to think of how to explain why she couldn't turn them away without offending him for prioritizing these people over his job.

"How can we help?"

She stopped in her tracks and turned to find Drew tying an apron around his perfect waist. He'd never looked so good.

"Seriously, these people need to eat."

"Um...that's so nice of you. I guess you could man the front and keep people calm."

Lori tied her hair back. "I've got that. You two stay back here and cook." She disappeared from the kitchen, leaving her and Drew alone to bake.

"I can make Southern Man Bars." He winked.

She threw her arms around him. "Thank you so much! I didn't know what I was going to do with all these people. You and Lori are life savers."

"If I'd known I'd get this much attention, I would've disabled the bus myself." He winked.

She slid away, heat rising to her cheeks. "Sorry. I was just—"

"Don't apologize. Promise me you'll tell me what I did so I can do it again."

She shook her head. "You're impossible. Wait... I didn't mention a bus."

Drew retrieved the mixing bowl and ingredients as if he'd been in her kitchen more than once before. "Nope. We heard you might need help, so Lori and I headed over here. Mary-Beth had Felicia and Stella working on the bus."

"Where's Roxy?" she asked.

"Ms. Melba is kitten sitting along with the other elders. Thelma even told them they could take her to the center if I was running late. Apparently, she's never enjoyed that much quiet and thinks the kitten is the best therapeutic tool ever." He chuckled. "I offered for them to keep the kitten, but Thelma said Roxy was like a new toy. Ms. Melba and the rest of them would think she's cute and cuddly for a while, but when it came to cleaning up after it, that would fall on her and she has too much to do already."

A part of her loved the fact this man knew all her friends' names and what was going on in the town. He seemed different today, a little more relaxed and interested in the people around them instead of just his show.

The crowd was loud and boisterous with relief from the cold and hunger. Her heart filled with the feeling of providing for others again. "If I could have crowds like this, I'd be able to expand into the shop next door that closed down."

"Is that something you want?" Drew put the pan on the top of the stove while she concentrated on some more scones.

"I've always dreamed of expanding into specialty cakes, seasonal pie club, and even breakfast sandwich items on home-made bread. I know, I know, there aren't enough clients in the area to necessitate such things. Stella mentioned that I could offer an online service for the pie club, but I don't know."

"There are plenty of patrons in Los Angeles. I know they'd flock to a shop like this."

"Maybe, but I doubt those healthy, seaweed-eating types would put real sugar in their bodies." She winked at him.

"Despite elder small-town belief, not all city folk eat salads three times a day." He brushed hair from her eyes and tucked it behind her ear. "There, now you can see."

"You mean that my hair out of place bothered you." She chuckled. "I jumped into full-on cooking before I even took a second to tie my hair back."

He took her arm, slid the hair band from her wrist, and then stepped behind her. His fingers raked through her hair, sending ripples of shivers down her back. With a determination to focus on the task at hand instead of some man who would be gone in a few days, she picked up the cinnamon to add to his Southern Man Bars.

"You sure you want to put that in?" Drew placed a hand over hers to stop her movement, causing an eruption of pulse-thumping music in her ears.

"Boy, you have one success and you think you're a baker."

"I have no delusions about being good in the kitchen, but even I don't think there's supposed to be cayenne pepper in the bars."

Heat flooded her cheeks, neck, arms. "Right." She forced a long breath and capped the cayenne pepper before any damage could be done. "I'll get the cinnamon."

She rushed to the pantry and fell against the wall. One breath. Two breaths. Her hands shook and her chest tightened. She hadn't felt this way since...well, never. The butterflies, sweaty palms, over-energized love mythology she'd seen on television and read in fairy tales that she'd thought was a lie. Until now. And now wasn't a good time.

"Reinforcements are here." Felicia's voice was like water at the end of a marathon. Cool, refreshing medicine to keep her from collapsing. "I brought in chairs from the church. Where's Carissa?"

"Pantry. You might want to check on her. I think all these people were a shock."

Shock to her? No, not the people. Him. His touch.

Felicia rounded the corner and her eyes shot wide. She shuffled inside and shut the door behind her. "What's wrong? Did that man upset you? I can get Stella to take care of him."

Carissa shook her head. "No. It's not that. He didn't do anything, not intentionally."

Felicia rubbed her arms the way she did the time that she'd overheard her parents talking about leaving Sugar Maple. "I don't understand. Is this project too much? Did we push you too hard to make this work?"

"I don't know." Carissa felt like the pantry tilted under her feet. "No way I want to feel this way. I need it to stop. To go away. Far away."

"What to go far away?" Felicia took a step back and eyed her and then the door. "Drew?"

Carissa couldn't talk or even form a thought. "I never wanted to meet a man who made me feel anything. Not after. I mean, I don't have room in my life right now. And not him."

"Stop. Take a breath, hon. Are you saying you like Drew Lancaster?"

"No." Carissa threw her hands up in the air. "I don't know. It's different than it was with Mark. I'm overreacting. There isn't anything between us. Drew was right. I'm overwhelmed with everyone being here. That's why I reacted to his touch that way."

"He touched you?"

Carissa's heart slowed and the tightness in her chest relaxed. "I overreacted. He only pulled my hair back from my face so it wouldn't get into the food. And my body did this crazy, over-loaded circuit thing. Like I was running the stove, mixer, and microwave before Stella helped redo the electrical in here."

"Oh." Felicia broke out in an I-see-what-you're-not-saying grin. "Well, you're probably right. I mean, you barely know the guy."

"Right."

"And he isn't even a nice guy."

"He is. I mean, more than I would've thought. Did you know he rescued a kitten?"

"I heard, but it was only to win the town over."

"No, actually, he's totally attached to Roxy. He plays with her despite the fur."

"Despite the fur?"

"Yeah, he doesn't like lint and dust and stuff. He's kind of…obsessed."

"One of those, huh? Jacqueline told me he could be rude."

"Jackie is rude, not Drew. He's always polite. I mean, he just jumped in here to help, despite the fact I'd promised to meet with him and Lori."

Knock. Knock.

"Is everything okay in there, ladies? Do I need to call Charlie? Are you locked in there?"

He'd even remembered the fire chief's name. "Be right out. Felicia's helping me figure out what I did with the cinnamon."

Footsteps padded away, so Carissa straightened her apron and tightened the band in her hair, remembering what his fingers felt like on her neck. "I better get out there. Thanks for bringing the chairs."

"Sure. I'm glad I could help you figure out it was just an overloaded circuit thing."

Carissa turned the knob. "Right, and that, too. Just keep my crazy meltdown between us, okay?"

"Sure. I won't tell anyone, not even if it's an I-have-feelings-for-a-guy-but-I'm-too-scared-to-admit-it thing."

CHAPTER FIFTEEN

THE MORNING FLEW BY FASTER than Drew had planned, and they were running out of time to discuss the shoot, but no matter how hard he tried to focus on the job, he found himself focusing on Carissa. She was passionate and unpredictable and distant.

Lori tapped her watch. "We've got the call with Knox. I'll go back and take it at the inn while you stay here and review the details for Friday."

Drew nodded, but this entire project had gotten out of hand. If only he could put it back on track and show Carissa that she was the woman for the job. Unfortunately, he got the sense that she wasn't even happy he was in the room.

"Talk to her," Lori whispered. She slid on her coat and patted him on the back. "If you did something wrong, apologize. You know, for the sake of the project and all," she said with a dip in her voice and an exaggerated double thumbs up.

"Don't you have a call to take?" he asked.

"Don't you have a girl to win over?" She grabbed her stuff and left along with the last of the patrons.

The tour guide returned to settle the bill, and Drew listened in while he wiped down some tables until every last sticky spot had been scrubbed clean and the crumbs were in the trash.

"This disaster turned into such a treat. My company wanted me to tell you that this town is going to be a stop on our way to Nashville. We'll want to work out a deal to have those delicious treats and coffee waiting once a month. Our clients are raving, saying this is the best place they've visited in the south. The mayor even greeted them, and all the townspeople made them feel like family."

"That's what we're all about in our town. Family." Carissa shook her hand. "I look forward to working with you."

Drew draped the rag over the sink and cornered Carissa before she had a chance to get away. "Can we talk?"

"Sure. Let's talk while we clean up. I need to get the dishes done." She put two feet between them and wrung her hands.

"Lori and I did them while you were settling the bill with the tour guide." He took a step toward her, just to test the waters. She darted around the corner. The water was frigid.

"Okay, well, I need to get all the ingredients sealed up and put away."

"Done. I may have alphabetized your spices so you wouldn't have another oops with the cinnamon. I hope that's okay. If I overstepped, I can put it back the way it was."

"No, that's fine. I'll just put away the food."

"Done." He cornered her behind the counter and touched her forearm, but she reached up and pulled her hair free. "I'm sorry."

"For what?" She blinked at him.

"For whatever I did to make you want me to leave."

"I didn't say I wanted you to leave." Carissa untied her apron and hung it on the hook.

He followed suit. "You didn't have to. You've been staying two steps out of my reach for the last two hours. I know I offended you, but I don't know how. If you could tell me, then I could make sure I don't do it again."

"You didn't do anything at all." She returned to the storefront and scrubbed the tables he'd cleaned. "No worries. Our business hasn't changed."

He wanted to tell her he wasn't talking about their business, but he needed more information before he swam deeper into those dark waters. "Then why are you avoiding me?" He nudged her to face him. "If it's about the photo shoot on Friday, I promise I did everything I could to have it focus on Jacqueline only, but Knox has his heart set on you. I thought by sharing the segment, it might make it easier on you."

"I know. And I appreciate that. It's just, I don't want to be in the spotlight at all. I remained at this bakery all these years for a reason. I didn't want to have attention or connect with anyone but my town family. And now…"

"And now?" Drew took her hand. "What are you saying?"

"I'm saying that putting myself out there is frightening. The last time I tried to have a life beyond here, it was a disaster. Opening myself up like that again is cripplingly difficult. Especially when it's…possibly someone…something I could—"

"You could?" He squeezed her hands to encourage her to continue. Wanting to know what she was thinking and feeling. For once, he didn't want distance, he wanted to know more, explore more with this woman.

"Nothing." She retracted from him. "I know I said we'd meet today, but I didn't know the bus would be here. I've got to get to the courthouse for a meeting and then help Stella with something at the garage."

He didn't want to go. Not like this. Not when he knew she had more to say to him. "We need to talk, Carissa." His pulse revved, his stomach tightened. "Not just about the project."

Her eyes snapped to him, and that's when he saw the fear. He'd always been able to read women and avoid any mess, but with the woman in front of him, he wanted to be elbow deep in flour and conversation. He wanted to know more about her and to spend time with her. "I want you to know that I'm not the man this town thinks I am." He dared to step closer to her and was thankful when she didn't retreat behind the counter again. "Something about this town, about you, has me caring more about the people here than about the job getting done. That's a dangerous thing for a man in my position, but I won't stop."

She grabbed onto the counter as if to remain standing. "Care?"

"Yes, I do. I'm not sure what that means right now, but what I do know is that I'd like to explore things further. If you knew how opposite that is from my norm, you would be shocked."

Silence filled the room between them, neither daring to speak, and for once he didn't want to talk about anything, or plan anything, or organize his thoughts. All he wanted to do in that moment was to kiss Carissa Donahue. The disorganized, unpredictable woman he worked with who could ruin his career and his perfectly constructed world flaked off his dried-up painted wall he'd constructed years ago.

The door flew open, sending Carissa scurrying away. Mary-Beth stopped in her tracks with wide eyes. "I came to see how you fared, but I'm leaving now. Sorry."

"No, stay." Carissa turned her attention to wiping out the display cases. "Mr. Lancaster was leaving so he could take a call from Knox. They need to work out the details. Hopefully Jacqueline will be the star of the opening segment."

In that moment, he wanted to urge Carissa to open her mind and heart to the possibility of a life outside her bakery. On a segment that would win America over the way she'd won him over and to open to the possibility of something more with him. But he saw in the way she turned her back to him that she wouldn't, and the more he pushed, the more she'd run. The only thing he could do was let her go if that was what would make her happy. "Don't worry about the segment. I'll make it work with Jacqueline. No need to put you through any more."

"I don't want to be difficult or cost you your job." Carissa stopped scrubbing and looked at him with her deep green eyes with the yellow highlight.

"Don't worry about my job, and as for the project, trust me, Knox will love Jacqueline. You're off the hook, Ms. Donahue. I wish you the best." He turned on his heel and left the bakery and any possibility of the crazy idea that Carissa was the woman who could give him a real heart. Now, he needed to go fire Lori for putting the idea in his head.

CHAPTER SIXTEEN

THE QUIET AFTERNOON sounded like a punctuation to Carissa's loneliness. The morning had been full of life, baking for people, watching their bright faces, and listening to their thanks and praises. And there was Drew. He'd remained by her side all day, chipping in baking and cleaning. The man she'd pegged as uppity and difficult brought more softness to her than she'd felt in over a decade.

His touch made her feel like a fresh-out-of-the-oven chocolate chip cookie. Warm and gooey on the inside with an aftertaste of homey joy.

Standing in the middle of the bakery, she began to dream of possibilities. The kind that were dangerous and scary. The kind that could shatter her world when she didn't expect it.

The front door opened, startling her from her musings. In stepped Jackie with her laptop bag, high heels, perfect hair, and Blue Ridge Mountain–sized attitude.

Shock of her ex-best friend on her turf caused a surge of overprotective, this-is-my-space anger. "What are you doing here?" She tried to soften her tone, but they'd agreed a long time ago on their businesses being off-limits to each other. It had been Jackie's idea when she returned to Sugar Maple. Probably her way of making sure Carissa didn't keep reminding people of why she'd run off in the first place, since people of Sugar Maple valued honesty and friendship.

She ignored Carissa's question and sauntered into the center of the bakery as if she belonged. Her gaze traveled over the wood panel and exposed brick walls, the display case, and the bistro tables. One finger at a time, she removed her gloves. "Quaint. It's perfect for *your* shop."

"Get to the point. I have work to do."

Jackie did her hair flip, snicker move before she set her bag on the table. "I came for a chat. And to offer you a solution to get out of the Knox Brevard project."

"Maybe I want to be a part of it after all." Carissa thought about amending her statement or smacking herself for saying something so idiotic, but Jackie brought out her crazy.

"Please." The way Jackie rolled her eyes ignited something inside Carissa.

"What is that supposed to mean?" She straightened and snugged her apron straps up over her shoulders, ready to go into a baking escape.

Jackie's eyes faux softened, as did her plump lips. "All I mean is that you were born for this, not the public eye. You deserve to have your peace and quiet here. I want to help you avoid public humiliation."

"You want to help me?" Carissa laughed, a hysterical, you-are-insane kind of eruption of bubbling emotion. "Like you helped me with taking my fiancé away?"

"You weren't engaged yet," she snipped but then recovered with another hair flip. "Listen, I know we have a difficult past, but I still care about you. We were once friends."

"Friends? I'm not sure that was ever true. Sure we hung out, but let's face it, you thought you were better than the rest of us from the time we were in third grade and James Mallet chose you to sit next to at the school picnic."

"That was so long ago. You're not upset about that. We both know that you hate me because Mark wanted out of this town as much as I did and I provided him an escape route."

Carissa took in a stinging breath. "You stole the man I was to marry away from me."

"He went willingly." Jackie stood chin to eyes with Carissa as if she actually had a point. "All I'm saying is he had a choice. Now I'm giving you one. From what I've heard, if you back out, Drew has to make it work with my dress business, and we all know that I'm the one who needs to be the representative of this town. The town's struggling, and I have the experience and, let's face it, the personality to win viewers over. This is a no-brainer. And again, you get to escape the public spotlight. Something you've always hated." She picked up her purse and her gloves. "I'm glad we were able to chat. You should go tell Drew Lancaster that you want out and then everything will be fine."

"You're right. Mark did have a choice." Carissa fought the lump rising in her throat and the sting in her eyes. "And I have a choice now."

"Great." She slid her gloves onto her hands and headed for the door.

"I'm in the project, and the great Jacqueline Ramor is out." Carissa rounded the table and reached Jackie before she finished spinning on her spiked heels.

"You're making a huge mistake. How could you be so selfish? I know you hate me, but this isn't about us. The town needs this win."

"You don't care about the town. This is about you." Carissa swallowed the anger, the hate, the years of torturing herself for not being good enough for Mark to choose her, but she had let him go without a fight. Deep down, she had been relieved that she wasn't marrying Mark. It was easier to face that her one and only true love ran off with another woman, but it wasn't easy to face her true friend running off with her man.

"It doesn't matter why. Drop out," she said with a slight shake in her voice.

"No, not this time." Carissa untied her apron, invigorated and full of determination. She slapped her baking armor down on the table next to her. "This time I'm good enough. I'm the right person for this, and I'll be the one to help my town." She grabbed her coat, her keys, and her hat. "And this time I win. I win the project and the man. Now if you'll excuse me, I have a date with an Executive Production Coordinator to plan my segment."

Carissa opened the door and waited for Jackie to catch up on the conversation. She stood there with mouth ajar and bag swinging from her arm until she blinked twice and faced the door and the truth. Not that she'd believe it.

"You're making a huge mistake. I'll be the one in the end with the segment *and* the man." Jackie stormed out into the first real snowfall of the season.

There wasn't time for Carissa to second-guess herself. She needed to go find Drew and tell him not to report to Knox that she was out, but that she would be the only segment. She slammed the door shut, locked it, and hotfooted it across the town square. Head held high, pulse racing, she kept her eyes trained on the building that once housed the man of her past in order to find her future.

Out stepped Lori and another man she didn't recognize. Was that Knox Brevard? Was Carissa too late and she'd actually have to battle it out with Jackie on screen? If so, would Carissa stand a chance?

The man opened up a trunk and took out a large bag and a camera. A video camera. A camera she'd have to face when she committed to this project.

Her chest tightened as if the temp had dropped twenty degrees and she was on Mount Everest instead of in the Blue

Ridge Mountains. Snow fell hard, distorting her view of Lori and the man, but she managed to see them both go inside. Her pace slowed, her heart slowed, the world slowed. That peaceful, quiet, winter storm sound descended, where all life was gone beyond the blanket of white rain.

She stopped and collapsed onto a cold, icy bench at the edge of the road. What had she done? Could she really pull this off? A hand on her shoulder drew her from her fear. She turned to find Stella, her good and dependable friend. "I saw Jackie enter your bakery and then storm off. What happened?"

"I said stupid things. I'm doing the project. I have to make this dessert that's photogenic, and I have to speak on camera, and I told her that Drew was mine. Drew isn't mine, we had a moment, but nothing real. I probably imagined it. I mean, what would a man like that see in a small-town girl like me? And me on camera? Stupid. Stupid. Stupid."

Stella sat by her side. "Sounds like the most intelligent thing you've said in years. This is the first time that I've seen the old Carissa. The captain of the volleyball team, debate club, literary nerd who used to make me want to be sick. You were perfect in every way. You dated the star quarterback, ran cross country, straight As on every report card. We were all so jealous of you. Especially Jackie."

Carissa focused on sucking in air as if someone had given her a toddler straw to breathe through. "What are you talking about?"

"That's what made it even more nauseating. You didn't even know how amazing you were. A humble, sweet, smart, athletic, beautiful woman who was voted most likely to win over the world never saw the competition. Jackie loved you and hated you for years. She wanted to be you. Now she is you, except for the humble and nice part."

Carissa swiped snowflakes from her eyes. "You're crazy. I've always been disorganized. I would forget my homework, lose my shoes, forget my money."

"That only made you more real." Stella pointed at the building in front of them. "I think it's time you found your old self, girl. I, for one, miss her. Just don't tell her I said that because it'll go to her head."

Carissa wrung her hands, trying to keep warm and thinking about her possibilities. "I don't know. I'm not that girl anymore, if I ever was her."

A wind sent the last of the dead leaves from the overhead trees. They'd be gone until spring. That's how Carissa had felt, like she'd lived in hibernation for so many years and now she'd woken up. Only, the world had changed and she was lost and confused. "I don't know. If I'm being honest, Jackie will win. I'm not real competition for her."

"That's because you've never fought to beat her. If you're completely honest with yourself, you gave Mark to Jacqueline. She didn't win. You let him go."

"What?" Carissa snapped to attention, but at Stella's nod, she knew her words were true to some degree. "I...maybe, but this is different. Drew isn't the quarterback of a small-town football team. He's the quarterback for a famous internet show. One that reaches millions. A man with perfect hair, strong and soft all at the same time. A person who is used to big-city life, not our tiny town, and I don't want to leave Sugar Maple. I never did. This is my home."

"And that's why you let Jackie steal Mark away. Because you knew if you married him, you'd be forced to leave."

Carissa studied her boots covered in crumbs and snow. "I know I can't remain hidden in my bakery, but I don't want to put myself so far out there that I make a fool out of myself and the town."

"You won't," Stella said in an uncharacteristically sweet tone. She cleared her throat. "But if you don't go home, clean up, figure out what you're going to make, and storm into that man's personal and professional life, I will run you over with my 1957 Chevy."

"You got that running?" Carissa asked.

"Nope, but this might just be the motivation I need." Stella pulled her from the bench and shoved her toward her apartment and bakery. "Go. And Carissa… That man would be insane not to see how amazing you are. You just have to believe it yourself."

CHAPTER SEVENTEEN

THE DINER BUSTLED with more activity than normal. Drew only hoped the noise wouldn't wake Roxy after her three-hour obstacle chase through the office. She stirred in the bag at his side.

The senior center bus pulled up, and Ms. Gina, Mrs. Malter, and Davey pranced inside. For the first time, Davey acknowledged him without a glower or scowl.

"Morning." Drew raised his coffee cup in a toast.

Davey nodded, tipping his cap to him. If Drew had to guess, that was southern for a respectful good morning.

Lori laughed.

"What?"

"You look like you scored an A on a test. I can only imagine how competitive you were in college." Lori looked over the one-page, cardstock menu with a maple leaf at the top.

"It cost me my first college girlfriend. She didn't appreciate me telling her that she could do better than a ninety if she skipped her sorority social to study more."

Lori gasped with an exaggerated eyebrow raise. "You dated a sorority girl?"

"That's what you got out of that?" Drew set his menu down, deciding on eggs and bacon without asking for anything special. He suspected that he'd get knocked down on the respect list if he asked for an egg white omelet and turkey bacon.

The young waitress who had to be barely over fifteen bounced up to their table. "Mornin'. I heard strangers were in town. Are you the big-time producer person from Los Angeles?"

"No, I'm just the event planner, and this is my assistant."

Lori quirked a brow at him and buried her face behind her menu.

"Knox Brevard will be joining us on Friday to supervise the first test segment filming."

"Welcome all the same," she said, as if despite their failings, they were still invited to eat in the diner. "Ohhhhh, how cute is he?"

"He's a she, and don't tell Doris she's in here, okay?"

She put her finger to her lips and turned her hand, mimicking a key lock.

"Your secret's safe with me. What can I get ya'll this morning?"

Lori set her menu down and patted the top of it. "Would it be too much trouble to ask for an egg white omelet and dry wheat toast?"

The young girl with "Shirley" on her name tag scrunched her nose. He could almost hear her thoughts of *that's the grossest thing I've ever heard.* "Guess we better order some avocados. I hear all you westerners like avocados and healthy stuff." She scribbled something on her notepad. "I think the cook can figure out how to separate eggs. If not, I can show him. What can I get you?" She looked to Drew.

"I'll take the number four." He returned his menu to behind the napkin dispenser.

She smiled, showing overbleached teeth with a chip in the corner of her left front incisor. He forced his gaze to her eyes to avoid obsessing about the difference in balance of her smile. "Sure thing, sir." She curtsied like she was addressing the prince of Los Angeles.

Once out of earshot, Lori leaned over the table and dropped her fist with a loud thump. "You little—"

"Careful. You might offend someone here. They don't like your western kind of talk." He met her lean over the table. "I heard from Ms. Gina that you were caught saying a potty word in the coffee shop the other day. Not a good way to win over the locals, you know." He sat back and stretched as if he'd relaxed at home.

This place did feel like home. More so than his apartment in LA.

"You set me up. Okay, you made your point. You've risen to the challenge, and you were able to overcome your militant ways to blend in with the people while I stick out like a screaming baby in a 'Le Pierre' during a seven-course wine-pairing dinner."

He scratched his chin and realized he hadn't shaved this morning. How many years had it been since he'd skipped shaving for even a day? "I didn't set you up, but I will confess that I enjoyed seeing you squirm."

"Sure you didn't. Pleeeease. I've known Drew Lancaster since he was fresh out of the military and ready to own the world with his wisdom and control. You're playing. You want me to believe that you're really falling for this town and a certain girl so that you'll win that bet and I'll have to call my father for that job."

His skin heated and he lurched forward. "Shh. Don't talk so loud."

"What? You scared I'll blow the bet about you going on a few dates with Carissa to score the job of your dreams?"

"Stop," he said in his deepest, I'm-warning-you voice.

"Good morning. I'm glad I caught you both here." A voice none other than the wannabe socialite Jacqueline Ramor jolted him to the core.

He'd been so engrossed in their conversation he hadn't seen her approach. This woman was like fungus. Every time you thought you'd gotten rid of her, she'd reappear. Fear turned up his skin temp to fire hot. "Ms. Ramor, what can we do for you?" His tone was harsh, so he tried to soften it, but it caused his throat to tighten. "Are you ready for your international debut on Friday?"

"That's what I wanted to speak with you about." She slid into his side of the booth, nudging him to make room for her.

The woman was relentless. He would usually respect a person who worked and manipulated to get a job, but not now, not here. It seemed wrong in a place like Sugar Maple. How had she grown up here? And his biggest question was, had she overheard their conversation?

"Carissa's working so hard, and I'm concerned about her." Jacqueline tipped her chin down, allowing her hair to fall over her cheek. He'd avoided actresses after one date with one when he'd first arrived in LA. Their emotions were too much for him to handle on a day-to-day basis. Everything had to be a show.

"What about Carissa?" Lori asked, because he had no intention on engaging in such conversation.

"I'm afraid she's working so hard to help the town she's loved her entire life. You know she chose this town over her own family when they moved away. They've barely spoken in years."

"That's a special quality that should be respected," Drew said in the most relaxed tone he could manage.

Shirley returned with a pot of coffee, and he scooted his cup toward her. "Yes, please."

She poured it and curtsied again, but her eyes only skimmed Jacqueline and didn't ask her if she wanted anything. No love lost between them, that was obvious.

Jacqueline cleared her throat. "Yes, of course, but at what expense? I mean, isn't her health important enough for people to realize how much stress they are putting on her? I don't want her to suffer again. Not like she did before." Jacqueline raised one finger at the waitress and tapped her mug.

Lori took the bait. "What happened before?"

Jacqueline tucked her hair behind her ear in a Little Miss Muffet innocent way. "It's not my place to share her darkest secrets."

"Then you shouldn't," Drew snapped.

Lori traced the rim of her glass. "I understand. Of course we don't want to pry."

"Of course you don't." Jacqueline wanted to share the secrets of Carissa Donahue so badly she didn't even let Lori nudge her to the truth. "But the town doesn't understand by pushing her in this direction so that we can have a better future, she could have a nervous breakdown before filming ends, and where would that leave the town or your production?"

Lori sat straight, as if hooked and being reeled in, but Drew wouldn't allow it.

"I'm sure Mayor Horton, who took Carissa in when her parents left town, would never put her in a situation that would jeopardize her health, mentally or physically."

The corner of Jacqueline's mouth twitched with obvious frustration. "Yes, I agree. But she ran on a platform about improving our town circumstances by bringing in more business. She made a promise, and that was the platform she plans to continue with for her upcoming reelection—"

"Are you saying that Mayor Horton cares more about the financial situation of the town than the young woman she took in as her own daughter?"

Lori shot him a sideways, shut-your-mouth look. "I understand your concern. We'll speak with Mayor Horton and Carissa."

"If you think that will work, but they've already pushed her over the edge. I mean, she'd never agree to fly solo on this if they hadn't pushed her into it. You want a perfect recipe. Well, you've got one… A perfect recipe for disaster."

Jacqueline meant to scare them away, but his chest warmed at her words. Carissa had decided to do it? To be the heart of the first segment? He wanted to point out her cliché but decided that wouldn't help him convince Lori that this woman was full of evil and her only intent was to thwart Carissa so that she could have the spotlight. "So to be clear, Carissa has agreed to be the star of the first segment in order to save the town?"

"Yes."

He scooched into her, pushing Jaqueline unceremoniously out of the booth.

"Where are you going?" Lori asked.

"To find Carissa." He dropped a twenty on the table.

Jacqueline leaned into him. "I'm sorry to be the one to have to tell you all of this, but someone had to be the voice of reason. I wouldn't want your program to fall apart before you even filmed the first segment."

"I assure you, Ms. Ramor, it won't. Because we'll have the best woman for the job on Friday when Knox Brevard arrives."

Jacqueline puffed her hair. "Great."

He smiled and stepped closer. "Carissa Donahue."

CHAPTER EIGHTEEN

CARISSA STUDIED herself in the mirror. The aran knit patterns on her sweater ran straight from collar to waist. The dark maroon shirt underneath had the same amount of cuff turned up over each of the sleeves of the sweater. Her hair was brushed to a shine, straight, symmetrical on both sides of her face.

She took a second to apply lip gloss the way Mary-Beth would when she gave Carissa a makeover. The clock chimed, telling her she'd spent triple her usual amount of time getting ready and probably double any other time in her life.

Two more scans in the full-length mirror hanging on the back of her door before she finally decided she was presentable enough to face Drew Lancaster. If she hadn't already blown her chance to be the star of the first segment, then she wanted to look presentable. Beyond that, she wanted a date with him. The one he'd kept asking about since they met.

With one last twirl in the mirror that sent her ankle-length skirt into an umbrella shape, she checked her black-heeled boots to make sure there were no scuffs and then headed downstairs to her bakery.

Her stomach fluttered and her palms were sweaty, but she

needed to do this. Not only for the town but for herself. It was time to live instead of hiding from the world.

A double knock at the front bakery door made her pause and eye the back kitchen door she used when stocking and receiving deliveries. It would make for a perfect quick escape, but she couldn't do that. Not to anyone she cared about, which was almost everyone in town, so she snagged her coat from the rack and put it on before opening the front door.

Drew stood shivering, pink nose and cheeks, arms crossed over his chest. "Hey."

"Hey." She bit her bottom lip but forced herself to release it. No need to show her less-than-perfect habits before she landed a date. "What are you doing here?"

His gaze roamed to her pointed-toe boots and then back to the top button of her shirt. "I came to find you." His teeth chattered so loud, she thought he might bust a cap. She assumed they were caps because who could possibly have perfect teeth for real?

"Why?" She was so busy attempting to look put together, she'd forgotten her manners. "Sorry. Come inside before you freeze."

He bolted past her to the center of the room, far from the doorway. "Where were you headed?"

She removed her coat and tossed it on the chair at her side but then retrieved it and hung it on the rack. "To find you, actually. Please, sit. I'll make you a cup of hot tea, or do you prefer coffee?"

"I'm fine." He set his bag down on the table, and out popped Roxy, who darted under the table and ran circles around them.

"Then why are you holding that coat like you're about to choke yourself?"

He dropped his hands to his side and rounded the table to stand by her side. "Is it true?"

She blinked up at him. His face was tense, but his eyes were soft. "Is what true?"

"Jacqueline told me—"

"Don't believe everything that woman says." She tensed, her neck tight, fists clenched. "She'd do anything to be the star of Mr. Brevard's entire show."

"I have no doubt, and I wouldn't normally believe a woman like that. She is more suited to Knox than me, to be honest." Roxy decided his pant leg was a climbing pole and made it to his thigh before he retrieved her and held her to his chest.

A tickle of anticipation hopped up her spine. "I'm sure you find her attractive. Every man does."

He patted Roxy twice, set her on the floor, and then removed his gloves and tucked them into his pocket. "Not every man. I don't." He took her hand in his chilly, large, firm grip. "I'm a man who likes a woman with more than just beauty and determination."

She swore if her heart could smile, it was grinning like a kid in her bakery on free chocolate chip cookie day. "What do you look for in a woman, then?"

"I thought I looked for intelligence, beauty, and determination before, but not now. Not after I realized there were women, or at least one woman, who has so much more to offer."

She swallowed hard and tried to force herself to listen to him, to give him a chance. Not even Roxy, who had found the one string hanging from her skirt, could distract her. "And what is that?"

"A woman who has a servant's heart, who cares more for others than she does for herself. Still as beautiful as any woman, intelligent and capable, but more. Talented, graceful, and creative."

Roxy abandoned the string and climbed her skirt. She reached down and carefully tugged the unruly kitten off and set her back on the floor. "You mean disorganized and imperfect."

"I wouldn't use imperfect to describe you."

She worked hard to believe his words, to capture them and hold on to them until she surrendered to them, but it was harder than she thought it would be to give a man like Drew Lancaster a chance.

"Listen, I know you've been through a lot, but I can promise you there is nothing now, nor ever, that would make me want to be with Jacqueline. Which brings me back to what she said to me. I need to know. Are you going to do the segment? The one without Jacqueline?"

His eyes were wide, his chest puffed as if to brace for impact.

She squeezed his hand. "It's true."

He scooped her into his arms and swung her around. "That's great news."

Roxy meowed her agreement.

The room whirled around Carissa. Dizziness filled her head, and she clung to him to remain upright when her feet touched the ground again. "Does that mean I have the job?"

"Yes, the job is yours. I've already emailed Knox and told him that we are set, and on Friday he will see how fabulous you are." Drew stood a breath away from her, looking at her as if she was the solution to world hunger. "You do realize all the viewers are going to fall in love with you."

"I don't care about that." She shied away, unable to face such possibilities, but he caught hold of her chin and nudged her to look up at his bright, lost-in-your-gaze eyes.

"That's what makes you perfect." He nudged her chin higher and pulled her to him.

His full lips invited her closer, his touch warmed her body, his strength surrounded her, but her mind bolted. Bolted to a place of broken promises and lies and lost love. Love that she swore would never exist in her life again. Yet here was a crumb of possibilities that led down a narrow, winding, and complicated path.

Roxy hissed and tore across the store.

She pressed her palm to his chest. Her heart thundered, pulse hammered, breath caught. Dang, she wanted to kiss him, but she knew if she did, she'd be lost forever. Gone from the solid ground she'd stood on all these years, the one she'd built herself with the help of a dear friend on a solid foundation of trust and honesty. "We should keep this business. I don't want to muddy the waters any further." There. That sounded like a solid reason. She wanted to go on a date with him. To test the waters, not engage in a long journey. "You'll be leaving."

"Not for a long time. There are several segments to run. Things like this can take time. Lots of time." He cupped her cheek but wouldn't let her gaze go. "Carissa. I'm not that guy, Mark. I won't run off with Jacqueline."

His words meant everything, but could she trust them? Could she put herself in a situation that could break her again? And if so, would she ever be able to recover? But if she didn't take the chance, she knew she'd be missing out on something great.

"You can trust me." He closed the last of the distance, and his lips pressed to hers. Soft, tentative, but powerful. How could a featherlight brush cause chain lightning, energizing her overly combed hair to her booted feet? She surrendered to it. The passion, the anticipation, the possibilities.

CHAPTER NINETEEN

"I CAN COME to the bakery after I finish up with Knox on our afternoon call and help inspire you." Drew rounded the corner into the kitchen of the small apartment-turned-offices to avoid Lori overhearing his conversation again. She'd enjoyed teasing him about sounding like a teenager in puppy love too many times over the last few days.

She had a point. He hadn't ever been this giddy. Heck, he'd never even used the word giddy before.

"No, I think I need to focus, and you, Mr. Drew Lancaster, are way too distracting."

"Oh," he said, his tone sounding like that puppy love whine.

"It's not that I don't want your help. I'm afraid I can't concentrate on my baking when I have a devilishly handsome man nearby, not to mention his insane sidekick Roxy. I might put cayenne pepper instead of sugar in my special dessert."

Drew glanced over at the sleeping fur ball that purred and calmed him one minute and climbed the walls the next—literally. "We wouldn't want that."

Drew picked up Roxy and snuggled her to his neck. "I'll stop by this afternoon. Roxy misses you, and she won't be able to sleep tonight without seeing you."

"Roxy, huh?" She giggled. "I want to see Roxy, too. I'll text you later," she said before ending the call.

He slid his cell into his pocket before taking a deep breath and following the low voices into the main room. He closed the kitchen door and set Roxy on the back of the couch, where she snuggled right back into sleep.

Lori looked up over her laptop. "I need a coffee fix."

"I'm with you." They both snagged their coats and headed to Maple Grounds on the corner. At the bottom of the stairs, Drew stopped where the elders were hanging out. Ms. Gina was working on some knitting, and Mrs. Malter was sitting with some ladies playing cards. Davey wasn't around, though.

He waved and made a mental note to come back and ask about him. It wasn't like Davey not to be there. They hurried out the door and up the street through the frigid air blasting between the buildings. Inside, the warmth and the smell that promised an amazing pick-me-up invited them inside.

Mary-Beth waved from behind the counter. "Sit. I'll fix you both something and have it right out for you."

They settled into the corner table.

"So what, you win the bet."

"Shh. Don't say that too loud."

"Fine, but you do. If you're playing me, you're doing a good job. If not, I have one serious question for you…"

"What's that?" He hooked his coat on the rack along with Lori's and settled into his seat with his laptop in front of him.

Lori pushed the screen lower and leaned toward him to meet him eye-to-eye. "What are you going to do when this program is over?"

"Take that job in Los Angeles with your father you promised me." He winked, but when her expression didn't change from apprehensive to light, he sat back and crossed his arms over his chest. "You're not reneging on our bet, are you?"

"No. I'm not talking about the job. A bet is a bet, and you won. I'm not talking about the job." She shook her head. "I'm talking about Carissa, you goober brain."

"Goober brain? I think you've been in this town a little too long already." He smiled, remembering how he'd tossed and turned all night thinking about this exact subject. "Let's face it... If Carissa is able to pull this off, she'll be so well-known, she'll want to move out to the coast and open another shop. I'll be there to help. Finally, after these past few years, I'll actually have a job I want and a girlfriend I don't want to avoid."

"Girlfriend?"

"If I have to put a label on it." He tilted the screen higher and entered his code.

"Have you ever thought that she might not want to move out there?" Lori glanced toward the counter, where Mary-Beth headed their way.

"Please, of course she'll want to go. I mean, it's her big chance. She even said it was time for her to give up her past and work toward her future."

"And you think that future will be you and her in LA?"

"Sure, why not?" He offered his best sexy grin. "I mean, of course she'll want to be with me." He winked, but her words had knocked an idea loose that rattled around his brain. What if he was wrong? What if she didn't want to go to Los Angeles?

Mary-Beth placed their mugs on the tabletop and wiped her hands on her dish towel. "You know, I have to thank you both. I haven't seen Carissa this happy in years. This project is good for her."

"Yes, the project is good for her," Lori said with extra emphasis on the word *project*.

"And you, Mr. Lancaster. You've been good for our Carissa. I heard even Davey had some kind words to say about you last night."

A cell phone rang from behind the counter.

"Excuse me, please."

She rushed off, and they both began to work for a few minutes until Lori pulled out her cell phone.

"I guess I should get this over with. Maybe going to work for Dad won't be so bad after all. He is getting older, and I have been missing him recently." Lori paused by his side. "You know, unless you've changed your mind."

"Why would I do that? I mean, I care about Knox, but I'm done with his drama. I'm ready for a real gig on a real set."

"I'm not talking about the job."

Lori sauntered off and left him contemplating his options, but in the end, he only knew one thing. He'd waited a long time for this job opportunity, but he'd waited even longer for a woman like Carissa. No matter what, he'd figure out how to get her to go to Los Angeles with him. Good thing he had a little more time before Knox showed up and stirred more drama up around them. That was his specialty. Drama.

"Hey, man. Thought I'd drop in to check on things." Knox's voice crashed into him like a tank.

Drew turned to discover Knox with Jacqueline Ramor on his arm.

His heart sank with worry, his insides tightened and burned, churned, and ignited panic. Panic that if she had five minutes, she'd convince him to put Carissa out and Jacqueline in for the first segment. And that would mean Carissa wouldn't get her time to shine, which would mean she wouldn't have the fame needed to move to Los Angeles.

Nope. This wasn't happening. He'd make sure Jacqueline didn't steal anything else from Carissa. Not while he was around and could stop it.

THE SNOWFALL HAD SLOWED, but the temperature had dropped to the teens. Carissa stepped inside the warm space of wooden, glass, and iron tables, smelling the aroma of Sugar Maple and listening to the sound of the milk frother squealing. Not loud enough to cover the sound of Jacqueline's laughter, though. A sound that sent a North Pole chill down her spine.

A man with a chiseled jaw sat with his arms around her, Drew on her other side. They all looked cozy, like a *Friends* episode in the cafe. So cozy that they didn't even notice Carissa had entered the coffee shop. The man with them, who she assumed was Knox, smacked his palm to the table. "You are the one. Be ready on Friday."

Carissa's chest throbbed, and her mouth went dry. She clutched the collar of her coat tight and shuffled backward, running into Mayor Horton at the door. The café felt like a broken tilt-a-whirl in a horror film. "Sorry. I...I need to go." Her heart smacked, smashed, and splintered against her lungs. She flew out the door and into the center of town, attempting to catch her breath.

Cold, bitter air penetrated her lungs. She released a white puff, but the oxygen still felt trapped in her lungs. Mayor Horton appeared at her side, rubbing small circles on Carissa's back with her hand. "I know it looks bad, but we don't know."

She pulled another breath, feeling like she was playing tug-of-war with the air. "We do know. Jacqueline strikes again." The sting on her skin turned to heat. She forced her lungs to cooperate with one long, deep breath. Once she managed to gain her footing on the icy ground beneath her, she glanced over her shoulder, catching Jacqueline staring at her out the front window. The two men sandwiching her didn't follow her gaze. Drew stared at Knox, whose eyes were locked on his target.

"Listen, you don't have to do this. I can make sure that you're no longer a part of this. I owe you an apology. I thought this would help mend things between you, but it did the opposite. You look more broken now than you did ten years ago." Ms. Horton gripped her arm. "Please forgive me."

Carissa forced her gaze away from the scene in the café and faced Ms. Horton. That's when she knew the truth. "No, you were right. I do need this."

The wind sliced between them, sending their hair into a tizzy.

Ms. Horton blinked and shook her head. "I thought…"

Carissa chuckled. Her memory slid back to the day Jacqueline told her that she'd stolen her man and they were leaving town. At that moment, she'd backed away from the fight. A fight she didn't want to have. Not for Mark. "Perhaps Jackie did do me a favor all those years ago, but it was easier to hate her than admit that I'd made a mess of my life." She straightened her coat and gave a single nod. "Not this time."

Ms. Horton swung her fist in front of her body, giving a mock punch. "Good for you. Go fight for Drew."

"No, Drew will have to make his own choice. I'm going to fight for my bakery. I'm going to fight for my friends. I'm going to fight for you, the woman who is more like a mother to me than my own."

Tears formed in the corner of Ms. Horton's eyes. "You know I love you. All you girls are like the daughters I never had."

"I know. It's time for me to recover from what happened and live my life the way I want to, and I want to be a successful baker."

"But you hate being in the light. You despise attention. How will you handle all the publicity? I don't want to see you unhappy."

Carissa lifted her chin. "I never wanted to be in the light because I feared I'd outshine Jackie. Even after she ran away with my fiancé, I still hoped my childhood friend and I could make things work. I've taken a back seat my entire life, but not any longer. My mother was wrong. I am meant for bigger and better things than being a wife." She spun on her heels and headed toward her bakery. "Watch out, world. Here comes the real Carissa Donahue."

"It's about time!" Ms. Horton hollered after her.

There wasn't time to mourn over the loss of a man. It was time to bake, and that's what she did best. So she donned her apron, locked the front door so she wouldn't be disturbed, and worked and worked and worked. Ten amazing desserts rested in the display case by late afternoon, and it was time to unlock her door and invite the townspeople to give their honest opinion.

The smell of fresh pumpkin, maple, and cinnamon filled the room. It was a salve to her heartache.

She texted everyone she knew with a cute little graphic she'd created on her phone app with an invitation for free desserts. That should get some people moving. Even the knitting circle, the retirement home, the recreation office… She even texted Jackie, Drew, and Lori. This was business.

No, this was war. And she was armed with the rapid-fire delicious array of treats that would bring any combatant to their knees, including her prize mini cupcake with sparkling sugar adorned with an espresso bean on top, which housed an unexpected surprise of dark chocolate ganache inside.

She glanced over at the poinsettia leaf in the center of a cake bite with the Christmas tree dot in the middle and smiled. That would be added to her holiday month menu. For some reason, her creative brain hit all the major holidays: Christmas, Easter, 4th of July, St. Patrick's Day, and more. When she ran out of holidays, she moved to seasons.

The front door flew open. "Well, that was fast." She turned with a bright, welcoming smile and was hit with a Jackie buzz kill shot of glowering attitude.

"This is pointless. What're you thinking?"

"I'm thinking that it's time for me to stop holding back."

Jackie slammed the door behind her, causing the china plates to rattle. "Holding back?" Her gaze locked on to the display case. "You're insane."

Carissa untied her apron and plopped it down on the register. "Actually, I'm the most sane I've ever been. I see everything clearly now."

The room remained silent, yet she could almost hear the racing thoughts in Jacqueline's head the way her eyes did a Davey jig around the room before coming to an abrupt halt on the three-tier cake with ivy cascading down the side like Rapunzel's hair. Her face softened, not the kind where everything looks relaxed and happy, but more forced like a child trying to behave to get what they want.

She removed her gloves as if to bide time to consider her words carefully. Carissa remained leaning against the back cabinets, allowing her space to process.

"Listen, this is all lovely. We all know you're a talented baker, but this is more than that. We both know that you'll fall apart once that camera's here."

Carissa folded her hands in front of her. "No. I've never fallen apart because I didn't like the attention."

Jacqueline stomped her spiked-heel shoes. "You hate attention."

"True, but I can handle it. I chose not to be in the spotlight because that was what you wanted." She concentrated on her calm tone, knowing that people would arrive shortly. Yet, she was worried if she didn't say this now that she'd never say it. "I chose to take a back seat because our friendship meant so much to me. You were the sister I never had. The one that promised to be my forever family. Even when you tried to ruin my life because you couldn't take the fact that I was marrying the high school star and that I was getting all the attention in town, I didn't want to fight you. I don't wish to fight you now, but I will."

Jackie huffed. "I can handle a little competition. And that's what you think? That I stole Mark because I was jealous? I wasn't. And I didn't steal him. News flash… He came to me. He told me he was making a huge mistake and he wanted to leave. He ran away, and I went after him."

"What are you talking about?" Carissa heard the tremble in her voice. She swallowed and forced her words to be slow and controlled. "Listen, you can try to twist this any way you want, but the fact is that you left with my fiancé. And now, you're attempting to use your feminine tactics to win Drew over. He's interested in me, not you. And I'm the one who will be featured in the first segment. Not you. No matter how much you coo and flip your hair."

Jackie's lip twitched. She took two heel-clicking, echoing steps toward Carissa. "And that's why I never attempted to explain. You can get off your high and mighty judgmental horse or not. I don't care. But I'll be the one featured in this segment. I've held back long enough, trying to figure out how to mend the fences between us, but you divorced me a long time ago. Just like my parents divorced, just like this town divorced me. I'm tired of living where I'm not wanted. I need this segment to spin-off my clothing line, and I intend on securing my spot. So take a back seat, not-so-forever sister."

The room heated to sweltering. Carissa tugged at her sweater's neckline, trying to breathe. That was it. Jackie had thrown down her faux diamond–studded glove, and Carissa picked it up. She matched Jackie's two taps forward with her two comfy boat slides. "No. You won't."

"You better step aside, because if not, I'll push you aside," Jacqueline said with venom in her voice.

"Try it." Carissa dared one more step, ready for the flour throwing, hair pulling, round of childish smackdown they'd been holding off for too long.

"It's a bet," Jackie said flatly.

Carissa tilted her head, hunting for the answer to the question she hadn't asked.

"Drew and you. He made a bet with Lori that he could get you to go out with him. He isn't into you at all, so he'll be easy to steal."

Carissa balled her fists at her side, wishing she was in one of those TV women's wrestling rings instead of being a southern girl in a bake shop. "You're lying."

The front door opened, and a crowd flooded inside.

"Ask him."

Carissa forced herself to shove her desperate muddy words into the corners of her Jackie compartment, tucked in the back of her brain.

Ms. Gina and Mrs. Malter shuffled in with Thelma.

"Welcome. Thanks for coming." Carissa grabbed two china plates. "Please, have a seat, and I'll put together tasting plates for you. Be brutally honest. I need real input."

Ms. Gina gave her the you-know-I-will look.

"Here's your chance," Jackie said, pointing to the door.

Drew and the man she assumed was Knox entered. Jackie took the plates from Carissa's hand and shoved her forward. She continued, tucking her hair behind her ear and straightening her sweater. "Hello, gentlemen. Welcome to Sugar and Soul Bakery. Please, have a seat and I'll get a sampling for you."

Drew reached for her, but she recoiled. "I'll be right back."

She fled to the display case and hid behind the three-layer cake. Jackie scowled down at her.

"As I suspected, like always, you don't want to know the truth. You only want to be a victim." Jackie plopped a spoonful of spring tartlet that looked like a blob of algae.

"Move. I'll do that, and I'll serve them. Don't even try to sabotage me." Carissa carefully constructed a tasting plate that would impress world-famous chef Gordon Ramsay and sauntered over to Drew. "Here you go, gentlemen."

Drew snagged a plate and slid it toward Knox. "You're going to taste the most delicious, amazing deserts."

Knox flipped his hair and studied the plate. "None of this fits our theme."

"Theme?" Carissa asked.

"Yes. Fall. We're going to create a fall set in the square, and none of these desserts look like they'd fit our theme. Funny, you'd think that someone from a town called Sugar Maple would make a dessert that represented their mascot." Knox nudged the plate away and brushed past her. "I'm sure they're delicious."

Carissa forced her disappointment not to show. "I'll have something to you in the morning, Mr. Brevard."

Drew patted the chair at his side. "I only found out about the theme earlier or I would've told you. Sit. We need to talk."

"No." Carissa retrieved the plate. "I mean, I need to focus on this for now."

"Don't let Knox get you down. He isn't the most delicate person. That's probably why we've been friends for so long."

"I see." Carissa let out a long breath. "Listen, this might sound crazy, and I apologize for even asking this." She nudged the fork so it wouldn't fall from the plate and examined the dark espresso bean.

"Ask me anything." Drew set his fork down.

"It's silly, but Jackie said that you made a bet with Lori to take me out on a date." She waited for his laughter, but it didn't come. That's when she saw it, the fear in his eyes. Drew Lancaster had many expressions, but fear hadn't been one of them until now. Not even when he'd faced Davey that first day he'd arrived in town.

"It's true." Drew folded his napkin and set it down on the table. "Please, you need to understand that it was a joke."

"Yes, I get that now." Carissa snagged his plate and headed for the kitchen. She'd been the joke.

Drew raced after her, catching her at the door to the kitchen.

"Please, let me explain. It was a bet to get me out of this job. Out of this town."

"Good to know you don't like it here. I'm a joke and you hate my town. Got it." Carissa had to get away from him before the tears welling up inside escaped.

"That's not what I mean." Drew ran a hand through his hair and then opened his mouth again.

"Mr. Lancaster. It doesn't matter what you mean. All that matters is that I produce the most memorable and beautiful dessert possible. That's what this is all about, right? How to make something look good, even if it's sour inside."

CHAPTER TWENTY

DREW COULDN'T FOCUS on business for the first time in his life. He'd been so stupid, making that silly bet with Lori. Heck, he never thought it was serious.

He abandoned the bitter coffee he'd made and decided to try to find Carissa to explain one more time. Since she'd shut the doors to her bakery with a note out front—*Busy baking for the Knox show. See you soon.*—she hadn't answered the door.

First he'd find Carissa, and then he'd find Knox, his idiotic friend who was being side railed again by a pretty smile. That woman had convinced him that everything should be all about her in a matter of minutes.

Drew rubbed his forehead, trying to alleviate the dull ache that threatened to pound some much-needed sense into him at any moment. How'd his world spin out of control so quickly?

He'd always liked his office area to be peaceful and quiet, but this morning without the boisterous laughter of the elders and no sign of anyone on the street, he'd never felt so alone. He rubbed his chest to free the tightness he hadn't felt since leaving his brothers in arms when his enlistment was up and he knew he wanted to go to college.

He closed the door behind him, no longer feeling weird about not locking it, and headed Maple Grounds. The bitterness of the wind penetrated his coat, and droplets of icy rain slipped from his hair, down the back of his neck and the length of his spine.

The warmth of the coffee shop took the shivers away, but the expectant eyes of the townspeople weighed him down. Not only would he fail Carissa but everyone who mattered to her if he didn't fix this mess. Knox sat in the corner with Lori, and to his relief there was no sign of Jacqueline. Good. Maybe he could convince his friend that Carissa would come through and that she was the right one for the job.

"Good morning. You look awful. Didn't you sleep?" Knox relaxed in the booth, stretching and putting his arm behind Lori like a bad blind-date move. Lori shot him a sideways, don't-even-think-about-it look. He sat back up.

"Where's Roxy?" Lori asked.

"Sleeping. She had her morning run around the office."

Lori slid out of the booth with her coffee mug in hand. "I'll grab you today's coffee special. Don't kill him while I'm gone. He still signs our checks for now, you know."

"Don't worry about me. I'll get my own refill," Knox said loud enough to draw a few prying people to edge closer to their table. "Sit. Tell me why you look like you haven't slept in a month."

"It's difficult to sleep when I've been up all night attempting to figure out how to make you see that you're making a colossal mistake."

Knox waved him off. "You saw the baker's stuff. Nothing right for the Sugar Maple shoot."

"No," Drew said and didn't even feel guilty about it.

Knox leaned forward, resting his elbows on the table. "Excuse me?"

"This is one of your blind, crazy, impress-a-girl moves that will cost us dearly. Need I remind you about the mechanic?"

"That wasn't my fault. Who knew the girl was a thief?"

"Thief? She ran a car theft ring out of her garage."

Knox rolled his eyes. "This is about that chick."

"Her name is Carissa, and no. This is about numbers. That's part of my job. And if you want me to be honest, starting your first segment with New York–style fashion is a huge mistake. The idea of coming here in the first place was to show your softer side—a loving, caring side that people could relate to. Preferably about a business that doesn't car jack grandmas. Do you really think that big city fashion is going to do that?"

The espresso machine squealed, drawing Knox's gaze. "You think so little of me. We were brothers once."

Drew flashed back to Knox pulling him out of a burning building. "We are. And like most brothers, we disagree and argue."

The front door opened, and Mayor Horton stepped inside with a tall man at her side. Based on small-town gossip, he assumed that was Mr. Strickland, her fiancé. He'd make a point to introduce himself later, but for now, he needed to get Knox to see the right path.

Knox twisted his coffee cup around so his left hand could lift it with the handle, and he took a sip and then placed it back down. "I've made up my mind. The clothes are vibrant and will show better. The girl at the bakery hasn't shown me anything that'll work for a fall shoot."

"That doesn't matter. She's the gift to get you out of the doghouse in the public eye. Think about it. Jacqueline is the wrong choice. The one you keep making. I love you like a brother, but I want to smack you upside the head each time a beautiful woman walks in the door and you lose all sense."

"I'm not interested in Jackie. I was working the problem. You stated Carissa didn't want it, and then she did. I wanted a contingency plan, and I have one now. A good one." Knox chuckled. "You think so little of me, yet you're doing exactly what you accuse me of: choosing a woman over the project."

"What? That's not true." Drew shifted in his seat and looked for Lori, longing for that coffee.

"Isn't it? I've never seen you so turned around and stressed. Look at you… Your collar isn't pressed. There's a wrinkle in it. And look at your sweater. There are little holes in it from a cat. A cat. You've never even owned a goldfish. You've never wanted the responsibility of having a pet, not to mention the hairy kind. And now you have fur on your clothes."

He couldn't help but look, and to his shock, all of it was true. That wasn't important now, though. "Listen, the bakery segment screams small-town charm. We can even play off of it with original recipes for mini-segments, have her cook in an elders' home or at a town event. The possibilities are limitless. We can incorporate the small-town feel into everything."

"We can do a mini-segment showing small-town women shopping in clothes designed by Jackie, set up a small-town fashion show—"

"All great ideas but not relatable enough. Not for what we need at this moment to fix your career. Trust me, this is my job. I know what I'm doing."

"Perhaps." He scrubbed his face. "I tell you what. I'll let Jackie know to be ready and standing by on Friday morning. If Carissa doesn't show with an appetizing dessert that photographs well and fits the theme of our segment, then she's out and Jackie is in. Got it?"

Drew knew he'd taken the argument as far as he could, and if he pressed Knox too hard and made him feel like he was being cornered, the man would buck like a wild horse and stomp anything around him. "Agreed."

"Of course, you need to get to work. Only forty-eight hours until the photo shoot."

"Not an impossible task at all." Drew rubbed his forehead. "I'll have everything ready and the team here on time."

"If you can't, then we pull and we postpone until next fall.

There's a better segment in Colorado with a small ski town to do a winter wonderland shoot in."

Drew's stomach clenched. "I'll make this work." He left the table, grabbed the latte from Lori as they passed each other without a word, and went to Mayor Horton.

"Hello, Mr. Lancaster. How are you today?" She offered her hand.

"Fine."

Mayor Horton patted the man at her side on the chest. "This is Ray Strickland."

"It's a pleasure to meet you. I've heard great things about you." He shook the man's hand, knowing he had to get through the pleasantries before launching into work if he didn't want to come across as rude. "I need some help. I need some supplies for the shoot on Friday. I'll have Lori message you the list."

"That isn't much time. What kind of supplies?"

"Things we'll need for the shoot. Also, could you provide transport from the Nashville airport for our team that will be arriving Thursday night for the filming?"

"I can probably get the senior bus for that evening." Mayor Horton scanned his face with an inquisitive lift of her brow. "Is everything else okay?"

"I'm afraid that if Carissa doesn't come through, then Jackie will be the first segment. If not, Knox will pull the plug and we'll be heading to Colorado."

Mayor Horton squeezed Mr. Strickland to her side. "Don't worry. Carissa will come through."

"Thanks. Hey, have you seen the town elders? They weren't having recreation time this morning. To be honest, I'm used to Davey giving me a difficult time each day. I kind of miss it."

"The recreation building's construction is complete, so they moved back to the center, and Davey's at the hospital two towns over. I'll text you the address," Mayor Horton said.

"Hospital?" A shot of anxiety heated him to furnace temperature. "Why?"

A woman flew over and snagged Mayor Horton's arm. "You need to hurry. There's an emergency at the Red Hat Society Meeting. Glenda Jones refused Marcie Atwell entrance to the meeting."

"Oh no. Those ladies feuding again?" Mayor Horton snagged Mr. Strickland's hand and headed for the door. "Please excuse us."

"Wait, is he okay?" Drew asked, but their attention had moved on to other things.

Drew rushed over to the other table. "Lori, I'm taking the car. Davey's in the hospital."

"Who's Davey?" Knox asked.

Lori shoved from the seat. "I'm coming, too."

"No, I need your help with something else. Can you attempt to explain to Carissa the bet wasn't really a thing?"

"Bet? What bet?" Knox shook his head. "I leave you two alone for a short time and all this drama ensues."

"Seriously? Pot? Kettle?" Lori glanced down at him and then back at Drew. "How did she find out?"

Drew glowered at Knox. "I assume Jackie told her."

"Ouch. I'll try, but if I were her, I wouldn't accept any explanation." Lori tapped her coffee lid and gave him a sympathetic look. "A bet to win over a girl isn't something she'll get over soon."

"I know." Drew sighed. "Just try, please."

Knox stood and smacked Drew on the back. "And I thought I made dumb mistakes. You blew it, dude. This woman's got you turned every which way but forward. At least, that's what Lori said."

Drew didn't have the energy to argue, so he ignored Knox and headed for the car. Before he could concentrate on fixing all this mess, he needed to find out if Davey needed anything.

Lori followed him outside. "You do realize this is a first."

"What's that?" Drew clicked the remote and the car beeped.

"You're choosing a person over the job. Drew Lancaster, I think you're becoming a real human being."

Drew opened the door. "Don't tell Knox that. He'll never let me live it down. Somehow I need to fix all this, and quick. I'll be back after the hospital so we can get to work. There has to be a way I can make this work for Carissa. She needs this win."

Lori smiled. "Tall order for one man alone."

"I'm not alone. I have you, and if the town is still speaking to me after they hear about our bet, which I guarantee they have, we have the mighty power of Sugar Maple behind us. If I was a betting man, though I vow never to place a bet again in my life, I'd put my money on these people. I'd put my money on Sugar Maple."

CHAPTER TWENTY-ONE

THE OVEN BUZZED. Carissa dragged her aching feet and back to the stove for the twenty-second edition of the perfect, fall Sugar Maple treat. At first whiff, she knew she had something this time.

She placed the carrot cake on the stove to cool. The aroma of the spices and maple were a perfect blend. It didn't matter, though. It could be the best-tasting dessert ever, and it wouldn't win. Now was the hard part. The decoration.

No matter how much she stared at the powdered sugar, cream cheese, and spices, nothing came to mind. Perhaps a flower on top or fall-color frosting with gold and burgundy sugar dust.

Ugh, too plain. Too glittery. Too wrong.

Tap. Tap...tap, tap, tap.

Stella's secret knock offered a temporary respite from her dilemma, so she wiped her hands clean and opened the back door to find Lori standing with a proffered coffee. "How'd you get Stella to talk?"

Lori stepped in without an invitation. "It wasn't easy. I had to make her an impossible promise to find her a part for a 1957 Chevy she's been restoring."

Carissa laughed. "So that's what our friendship is worth to her."

She raised the cup to Lori. "Thanks for the coffee, but no time to chat. I'm on the verge of a breakthrough, and I need to concentrate."

Liar.

Carissa didn't like lying, but she liked talking about Drew even less.

Lori set her purse down on the counter and sniffed the carrot cake. "Wow. If you need a taster, I'm happy to volunteer. That smells divine."

"Thanks, but the camera can't capture the taste. Still, I needed to figure out the flavor before I could share it with the world." Carissa forced herself to look calm, brave, ready.

"You're going to do great. I can see why Drew has such faith in you." Lori shoulder bumped her.

"Right, Drew." Carissa took a large gulp of hot liquid that went down scorching, heating her throat and then her chest and finally her belly. "You won the bet. I went out with him."

"I didn't come to find that out. The bet wasn't a real bet anyway." Lori shrugged. "It was a silly agreement between friends."

"Agreement?" Carissa asked. Her muscles tightened at having to relive the humiliation that they'd bet on her to go out with Drew. "That he could get a date with me. If so, he could get a job thanks to your father. Yep, he told me all about it."

"Right."

"So if he got the date, you had to get him a better job," Carissa said.

"Sort of."

"That's a bet." Carissa abandoned the coffee at the spice rack and pulled out a mixing bowl and dumped two cups powdered sugar in it.

Lori cleared her throat and rounded the island to stop a few steps from Carissa. "It's not like that. You need to understand. Drew isn't a bad guy. Sure, he's a little on the cranky side, wants things done a certain way, but he's more small town at heart than you might think. Drew didn't grow up in LA or New York. He grew up in a place outside the city, more small town, like here. He was raised on family time, including going to his aunt's place on the weekends to help make almond butter and some funky German dessert he always talks about."

Almond? That was it. The missing ingredient. She'd add it to the frosting and a sugar-coated, roasted almond to the top of each slice. And then perhaps, in the center of the cake, she could put an edible maple leaf. That was it... Down-home, simple yet pretty, with its own character.

She yanked open the mixing bowl cabinet and pulled out a new bowl, and then she grabbed a baking sheet from below, almonds from her pantry, and plopped them all down on the counter. "Excuse me. I've got work to do."

Lori stepped aside, allowing Carissa to pass. "He's a good man. Please give him another chance."

Carissa forced herself to remain calm, focused, independent. "It doesn't matter if he's a good man or not."

"He didn't mean anything by the bet." Lori edged closer into her personal space, popping her concentration bubble.

"This isn't only about the bet. Drew Lancaster will never remain in Sugar Maple, and this is my home. He will never be committed to this place or to me, so there is no reason to pretend otherwise. We are wrong for each other. And I won't stoop to Jackie's methods to flirt my way into my spot in Knox's internet series."

"You're giving up?" Lori asked.

"No. Absolutely not. I plan to fight hard to secure my spot, despite Knox's desire to work with Jackie. I'll make this the most amazing, photogenic baked good ever to grace the world. The icing will glisten, and the cake will be fluffy and warm with two layers sandwiching a thick cream cheese filling."

"My mouth is watering already." Lori eyed the cake. "Do you want me to try it?"

"No. I want you to see when its ready for its photographic debut." Carissa eyed the doorway. "Now if you'll excuse me. I want to work until I get this right. Even if it takes all night."

Lori backed away but paused at the edge of the island. "You're wrong. You two are perfect for each other. I hope you see it before you chase him out of town."

She left with a click of the back door in a wake of unwanted thoughts, wayward feelings, a twinge of pain in her chest, and doubt. A perfect recipe for an unhappily ever after.

CHAPTER TWENTY-TWO

DREW RACED through the sliding doors to the hospital and collided with the front desk. "I'm looking for Davey."

Bleach and other caustic chemicals bombarded his senses, and he longed for the aroma of Carissa's bakery.

The receptionist looked over her glasses. "You'll have to be more specific than that."

He rubbed the back of his neck and worked to remember his real name. "You know. He's old, and tiny, and dances like a mischievous leprechaun."

"Are you feeling okay, sir?" She reached for the phone. "Perhaps you should have a seat and I can get someone to help you. You just need to calm down."

"I am calm." His voice echoed through the busy waiting room. Everyone looked at him. That's when he realized his hair was disheveled and sweat trickled down from his hairline. Not to mention the rumpled shirt he wore and sweater with the holes in it. "I promise you that I'm normally more put together than this. It's just that I'm working for this crazy man who loses focus each time a pretty woman walks in the room. I was sent to this small town with a bunch of crazy people—at least I thought they were crazy—so that I could turn Knox's reputation from the most hated internet personality who lost a third of his following due to one of many poor choices." He paced in front of the reception desk. "Then I met this woman, and a cat, and an old man, and they confused everything I've clung to all these years."

"Sir, I understand. I need you to remain calm." She lifted the phone to her ear and pressed a button.

He smacked his hands on the desk to get her attention. "You don't understand. How could you when even I don't understand? This woman is everything I can't stand. I'm put together, clean, neat, borderline OCD."

"Um, sure you are." She glanced down the length of him.

"Not now, but normally." He ran his hand through his hair. "She's disorganized and chaotic and distracting. Smart, independent, strong, and beautiful. You know the type of woman who makes you willing to do anything to get her attention?"

The receptionist placed the phone back on the cradle and smiled at him. "Yes, women can confuse us, but there is always an option. You don't need to worry. This crisis will pass. We're here to help you, sir."

Two men came around the corner and headed for him.

"Wait. I'm not crazy. I'm just looking for Davey."

"The little man who dances like a leprechaun despite being old, right? These two men know where he is, and they'll take you to him," the receptionist said in a soft, soothing tone.

Drew shuffled toward the front door. "I don't need that kind of help. Sorry, I didn't mean to disturb you. I'll call my assistant and get his full name for you. Then you'll know I'm not crazy." He slid his phone out, which bought him a second to think. The men stayed close by, though.

"What are you doing here?" Davey's voice sounded from his side like a beacon in his darkness.

Drew pointed at Davey. "That's him. He's the tiny dancing leprechaun."

Davey removed his hat and held it in front of his chest. "I'm what?"

"Do you know this man, sir?" one of the burly men standing nearby asked.

Davey nodded. "I know him. Not sure I can vouch for him, but I know him."

"Wait. He didn't mean that. He's upset with me. He must know about the date bet." He faced Davey. "That's what I'm here about. Not the only thing. I was worried when I was told you were at the hospital."

Davey smacked his lips and put his hat back on his head. "What's your intentions for Carissa?"

"Intentions?" Drew looked at the door, but for once he didn't want to flee from complications and drama and mess. "I want to prove to her that she is everything I've been looking for in a life partner that I never knew I needed. That she is perfect in her imperfections."

"What are you willing to do to win her over? Not that you deserve her." Davey narrowed his gaze at him.

"Anything. I'll do anything," Drew said without hesitation.

Davey laughed and did a jig. "Then follow me. I got just the thing."

The men backed off when they saw the tiny man dance.

"Told you." Drew shrugged. "Wait, I was worried. Why were you in the hospital?"

"I wasn't. I was visiting an old friend. I come here once a month," Davey said in an everyone-knows-that tone.

"Do you think I'll ever win over the town? I hate to face decades of sideways glares and snide remarks if I stay." Drew hurried after Davey. Man, that little man could move. Wait. Since when did he decide to stay in Sugar Maple? It didn't matter. He had. He'd been working in LA for years looking for what came next after his military service and college. He'd been lost and hadn't known it, but now... Now he'd found himself and what he wanted, and he wanted Carissa and this crazy little town.

"You do what I tell you, and you'll not only win over Carissa but the entire town by the end of tomorrow. Promise."

A hint of relief relaxed Drew's shoulders. "What can I possibly do to achieve that?"

Davey smiled like a villain. "How's your handwriting?"

"What?"

"Nothing. Nothing at all. Follow me. We've got work to do." Davey shuffled faster than a toddler after candy.

A nervousness took hold of Drew. "Wait a second. What are you going to do?"

"Where's your car?" Davey headed for the parking lot with a backhand wave over his head. "I don't feel like waiting for the old fart van to get here."

"I'll give you a ride if you fill me in on the way." Drew clicked the remote so he could remember where he'd left the rental.

"I ain't doing nothing. It's what you're gonna do to yourself. Time for you to tar and southernize!"

CHAPTER TWENTY-THREE

THE CLOCK STRUCK eight in the morning, and Carissa knew she had to face everyone, especially her own fears.

Stella held up the cake platter. "Let's go, girlfriend. You've got this."

Carissa put on her coat, hat, scarf, and snow boots to trudge out to the town square. She opened the door and discovered the entire square covered in fall leaves. Faux trees were placed around the square, and people hustled about tweaking things.

Stella whistled. "Wow. I didn't think it would look that good when I helped dump some leaves out of a truck this morning."

In the center of it all was a rack of colorful dresses. They were in golds and reds but not the right hues for fall. She lifted her chin and marched across the street to the center of town, where she met Ms. Horton and Mr. Strickland. "I heard you were back from visiting your family Mr. Strickland." Carissa hugged them both.

Knox strolled up to Stella. "Didn't think I'd see a girl like you carrying a cake plate. Thanks for your help this morning. You've got talent."

Did Stella blush? In all these years, Stella had never blushed.

"It wasn't anything, really," Stella said, her voice an octave higher than Carissa had ever heard.

Wait, was she acting modest? Stella was abrasive, cool—never modest, though. "You two know each other?"

"We met this morning when the leaves were delivered." Stella twisted the plate as if to look for the best camera angle.

"Met? The truck broke down at the edge of town. We were going to have to carry wheelbarrow loads to the square. We'd never had made the shoot happen today if it wasn't for this lady."

Lady?

"She saved this shoot after that no-good Drew disappeared on us. And after I'd given him one more chance to redeem himself."

"Disappeared?" Carissa asked. A flicker of worry took hold. She pushed it away. That man was out of her life before he was ever truly in it. There was no way she'd ever be with a man like that. No way. No how.

Lori stood over on the sidelines holding Roxy. That's when she realized he'd not only left her and the town but also the kitten he'd rescued. Not that it surprised her. Drew Lancaster wasn't a bad person. He just wasn't *her* person. He didn't belong here. This was her life, not his.

Jackie made her entrance with floating fabric and clicking of heels. "I'm sorry I'm late, but I wanted to make sure I looked perfect for you, Knox." She took him by the arm and led him away, leaving Stella and Carissa by the cake that Knox hadn't even noticed.

Laughter filled the square, and there were hoots and hollers coming from the other side of the table and cameras. A crowd formed, and Knox unceremoniously abandoned Jacqueline, who stood awestruck.

"What's going on?" Stella asked.

Carissa took her by the arm. "I don't know, but let's find out."

The crowd parted, showing a leaf and maple-covered Drew Lancaster.

"Dude, what are you doing? This isn't part of the shoot," Knox shouted at him.

"He got tarred and southernized, you goon!" Mrs. Malter shouted at him.

Knox sidestepped away from her. "You people did this to him?"

"No, I did it to myself." Drew lifted his chin, sending a leaf fluttering to the ground in front of Carissa's feet. On it read, *I will never bet on a date with you again.*

Carissa picked up the leaf and eyed him, scanning him from forehead covered in yellow leaves to his matching shoes. "I don't understand."

He stepped closer, and she could read more of them. *I promise to always appreciate our differences. I promise to always respect Carissa Donahue. I promise to work on my perfectionist ways.*

He placed his finger on a leaf at his heart. *If you love me, I will stay in Sugar Maple for as long as you and the town will have me.*

Stella pushed her forward. "What man is going to do that to himself if he's not serious? No man has ever done something like that to win over Jackie girl over there."

A rush of emotion at the realization that this man who didn't like sticky things, who wanted everything perfect, had covered himself in syrup and posted notes to prove he meant them. All to show her how much he cared. She blinked the tears away for a moment but then surrendered to them.

The town stood silent, waiting.

She lunged into him and his icky, messy, syrupy mess, pressing her lips to his. The leaves fell over her eyes and nose, but she didn't care. The world around her faded away, along with past betrayals, past mistakes, and past regrets. All she saw in front of her was a bright future with Drew Lancaster and the little kitten, Roxy.

CHAPTER TWENTY-FOUR

THE BRIGHT SPOTLIGHTS heated the kitchen beyond anything her oven ever achieved. Which baffled her, since she wasn't even really cooking. It was all prebaked and sprayed with shiny stuff and fluffed with things she didn't want to know had been added to her food.

Knox retrieved the premade artistic version of her dessert from behind the counter and set it on the counter with an air of superiority, as if he'd created it himself. "Doesn't this look delicious. I don't know about any of you, but I'm ready to dig into this now."

Carissa snagged two plates with precut pieces of real food and passed one to Knox. "Then dig in." She smiled and slid the fork tines into the cake the way they'd instructed her so that the camera could capture it without her hand blocking the view.

"Mmmm, this tastes beyond what I'd imagined. I think someone in Sugar Maple called your treats a welcome-home flavor. I didn't get it then, but I get it now." He set his plate down, and the camera moved in close. "If you want a taste of down-home goodness, click on the link below to order your own Sugar Maple Carrot Cake, as well as many other delicious desserts Ms. Carissa Donahue will prepare for you. And for now, we'll leave you with your own family, but we invite you back to this beautiful and friendly southern town, Sugar Maple. Until next time."

The lights cut off abruptly, and Knox leaned in. "Don't worry. They add the music and special affects later. I know. It's kind of anticlimactic at the end of all this work." He offered his hand. "It's been a pleasure. I'll admit that Drew was right. You were the perfect girl and business to focus on for this in-depth installment of this series. I believe my fans will love this episode."

She took his hand and began to think this man wasn't all about himself after all.

"I have to agree with Mr. Brevard. You were the perfect choice for this. You were fantastic," Jackie's sultry voice sounded, but Carissa's brain didn't understand her words.

Carissa wasn't sure if Jackie said that to look good in front of Knox, but she decided to assume the best. "Thank you. That means a lot to me."

"You know, I was thinking." Jackie shifted her purse from one arm to the other. "This reminds me of when we were younger, and at the end of the semester, we would all finish our exams, and then we'd hang out all night and binge on treats and talk about boys and watch a horror flick that would keep us up all night."

Carissa's heart filled with the memories. "I remember."

Mary-Beth bounced up with Felicia in tow. "Hey, I'm in. That's if Carissa can stand to be away from Drew for five minutes."

The camera crew broke down the equipment, so Drew joined them. He kissed the top of her head, sending threads of warmth through her limbs. "I have to work tonight anyway, but you promise to meet me for breakfast?"

Carissa held tight to him, never wanting to let him go. "Sure. Sounds great."

"Of course, I can't promise we won't crash your party in the middle of the night, right, Knox?"

Knox laughed. "Now that sounds like a plan."

"Hey, Stella. You in for a girls' night?" Felicia hollered.

Stella huffed. "If I have to, but there's no braiding hair or painting nails. Got it?"

Jackie held up her hands. "That was one time. How was I supposed to know you'd get so upset when you woke up the next morning?"

Ms. Horton snagged one of the plates they'd taken a bite from a few minutes ago while on camera. "Hey, would you bake this for our wedding cake?"

"You set a date?" all the girls asked unanimously.

Mr. Strickland with his devilishly mature good looks and charm leaned against the counter. "Next fall."

Drew offered his hand and shook Mr. Strickland's. "Congratulations."

Knox slapped Drew on the shoulder. "Hey, maybe it'll be a double wedding. Unless, of course, you're going to take that job in LA."

Carissa froze, every muscle in her body tensed. They hadn't had a chance to discuss their future plans with the segment's filming and all the work.

"I did secure a new job at the end of this series."

"You did what?" Knox's voice didn't sound like the TV personality tone that he usually did.

"That's right. You're going to have to survive on your own."

Carissa's chest hurt. Perhaps he'd visit often.

He turned Carissa in his arms and brushed her hair from her face. "It's an online job except for the travel to scout locations, so I can live anywhere. So, if you want me to stay…"

"Do you *want* to stay?

Drew smiled. "Why would I ever want to leave when I've finally found a place to call home?"

Her insides warmed at the way he referred to Sugar Maple as home. "I read somewhere that if I will love you, you'll stay. You wouldn't want to break a promise, would you?"

"No, never. I never want to let you down again." Drew pulled her into his arms and held her tight, as if promising he'd never let her go.

The End

ABOUT THE AUTHOR

Ciara Knight is a USA TODAY Bestselling Author, who writes clean and wholesome romance novels set in either modern day small towns or wild historic old west. Born with a huge imagination that usually got her into trouble, Ciara is happy she's found a way to use her powers for good. She loves spending time with her characters and hopes you do, too.

ALSO BY CIARA KNIGHT

For a complete list of my books, please visit my website at www. ciaraknight.com. A great way to keep up to date on all releases, sales and prizes subscribe to my Newsletter. I'm extremely sociable, so feel free to chat with me on Facebook, Twitter, or Goodreads.

For your convenience please see my complete title list below, in reading order:

CONTEMPORARY ROMANCE

Winter in Sweetwater County

Spring in Sweetwater County

Summer in Sweetwater County

Fall in Sweetwater County

Christmas in Sweetwater County

Valentines in Sweet-water County

Fourth of July in Sweetwater County

Thanksgiving in Sweetwater County

Grace in Sweetwater County

Faith in Sweetwater County

Love in Sweetwater County

Riverbend
In All My Wishes
In All My Years
In All My Dreams
In All My Life

A Christmas Spark

A Miracle Mountain Christmas

HISTORICAL WESTERNS:

McKinnie Mail Order Brides Series
Love on the Prairie
(USA Today Bestselling Novel)
Love in the Rockies
Love on the Plains
Love on the Ranch
His Holiday Promise
(A Love on the Ranch Novella)
Love on the Sound
Love on the Border
Love at the Coast

A Prospectors Novel
Fools Rush

Bride of America
Adelaide: Bride of Maryland

YOUNG ADULT:
Battle for Souls Series
Rise From Darkness
Fall From Grace
Ascension of Evil

The Neumarian Chronicles

Weighted

Escapement

Pendulum

Balance

Made in the USA
Las Vegas, NV
30 August 2022

54310844R00109